God and Country

God and Country

Book Two of the Tuesday Meltdown Series

Book 1 Tuesday Meltdown
Book 2 God and Country

Joe Hinds

Copyright 2023 Joe D. Hinds
ISBN: 9798378300143

This is a work of fiction; therefore, the novel's story and characters are fictitious. Liberties have been taken with the details of public agencies, institutions, and historical figures mentioned in the story, which serve as a backdrop. All characters and their actions are wholly imaginary.

Dedication: This book is dedicated to my wife Denise, the love of my life.

Contents

Acknowledgments   i

1 Exodus	Pg	1
2 Congregation	Pg	11
3 Loss	Pg	20
4 Oppression	Pg	33
5 Freedom	Pg	42
6 Need	Pg	52
7 Shelter	Pg	67
8 Help	Pg	81
9 Broken	Pg	88
10 Goodbyes	Pg	101
11 Trust	Pg	108
12 Wandering	Pg	130
13 Rest	Pg	153
14 Battle	Pg	160

Acknowledgments

I want to thank my loving wife Denise for being my North Star, my unwavering constant, who provides me direction. She was an invaluable help in the publication of this novel. My parents instilled in me a sense of ethics, for which I am forever grateful. Finally, I want to express my gratitude to my gracious Creator. He has given me so much more than I deserve and is my Purpose for being.

Chapter 1

Exodus

Hunter was gripping the passenger door for dear life as Paul flew the pickup over the crest of a southwest Iowa hill. The vehicle hit the road with a bone-jolting thud, causing the deer carcass between them to hit the roof. Luckily, Hunter was buckled in. He looked over to Paul, who was gripping the steering wheel maniacally. The crazed driver released one hand from the wheel and reached over to slap the dead corpse between them. "Stay put, Bam-bi!" Paul yelled out in a maddened sports chant, beating the steering wheel in cadence.

Behind them, two M998 Humvees made the same jump amidst a choking white dust being churned out from the Chevy they were pursuing. Hunter looked at the shotgun pushed up against the passenger door. That and Paul's deer rifle were not going to be much of a match against assault rifles and machine guns, Hunter thought.

"All of this for a stupid deer, right!" Paul yelled. No, actually, that was not quite accurate. It was the two firearms that were the big problem. The Department of Homeland Security made it very clear that all firearms, rifles, shotguns, pistols, were illegal. Between gun possession and resisting arrest, the two Clarinda natives could be facing severe punishment, perhaps even summary execution.

Paul looked over to Hunter and thumbed behind them to the rear glass of the vehicle. "I think we are going to lose them. Hang on this is going to be a big bump."

The vehicle crested the next hill, taking flight for a moment, then hit the ground. The truck's suspension popped, as if exploding.

"Oh, shit!" Had he realized those would be his last, Paul might have selected a more profound choice of words. In front of them was a semi truck packed with telephone poles. Paul swerved, corrected the truck from rolling, and flew down an embankment into a cluster of rather large cedar trees. A tree trunk caught the front driver's side of the pickup, effectively

God and Country

halting it from 45 mph in a second. Two bodies hit the front of the cab with a devastating, skull cracking effect.

Behind the pickup, one Humvee, then another cleared the same hill in a cloud of dust. Speeding blind, neither military vehicle saw the enormous wooden and metal obstacles immediately in front of them. The first hummer caught the long wooden poles through its upper windshield, crushing through the two occupants to the back of the vehicle. The second hummer slammed into the first, wedging it under the semi trailer. The telephone poles succeeded in almost totally penetrating the vehicle's cab, forming a sort of twisted, bloody vehicle kabob. This rendered the occupants of that second military vehicle quite dead.

In the pickup, Paul was also quite dead, having been thrown through the windshield. Eyes open in death, his face still held that same defiant shit-eating grin that had challenged both his friends and authority in life. Another dead body lay in the vehicle, its skull shattered, almost every rib snapped. Yet behind that body something else was quite alive.

Hunter awoke to find himself covered in the blood of a deer that had taken the deadly impact for him. "Thanks," Hunter thought whimsically. A very dead Paul seemed to express the idea of an encore as if asking "Now what?"

"Somebody cue the snare and hi-hat," Hunter responded silently, adding "Crazy fucker," to punctuate the end of this tragic comedy.

But, it was a good question. "Now what?" That was a question Hunter had been asking ever since the entire country collapsed. On a Tuesday afternoon in October, there had been a rush to his hometown's gas stations, with people bringing every container they could find. Next came a rush to the stores. The local LowVee was raking in the money and maintaining control until the electronic credit card system stopped working. People began to simply walk past the checkout lines, and the store manager wisely chose not to stop them. Then came the fighting at the stores when supplies began to run out. Long time friends and neighbors turned against each other over the last canned goods. The next day, the cell phone service stopped. Internet service and television broadcasting slowed then blacked out. The electric power stopped on that Friday. Then came a week of uneasy silence. A questioning fear: "Now what?"

    Following the advice of his grandparents, Hunter decided to move to their house two miles southeast of town. Hunter loaded up his suburban with clothes, blankets, and all the food he had. In the vehicle with him was his eight year old daughter Hannah, his wife Brittany, and a cold silence. Brittany had raised objections about moving, but that was nothing new. Brittany "raised objections" about most anything. Ever since the wedding, Hunter had lived in a state of torment. Brittany complained about their house, about his family, and mostly about Hunter himself. Hunter had married her for love; he wanted to make her happy. Soon, however, Hunter realized that was impossible. When Hunter insisted that his daughter go with him, her mother insisted on going with them.

    The family drove slowly down Washington Street. Going past the city square, there appeared to be some military vehicles on the other side of the courthouse. Although curious, Hunter was set in his decision to leave town and hoped to avoid trouble. He drove on, keeping his twelve-gauge shotgun in his lap just in case.

    Hunter shook himself back to the present and evaluated his circumstances. That same twelve-gauge Mossberg was still inside the truck door and seemed in good condition. How about him? There was a cutting pain on his face. Both legs seemed okay. Something wet on his forehead? Instinctively he reached up, blood. The movement caused the crushed carcass of the deer to slide down more on his lap. Unlike the other occupants of the vehicle, Hunter seemed miraculously uninjured.

    Dust still hung in the air along with a silence. Had the DHS agents simply left? He reached for the door handle, pulled it, and was greeted with a "ding-ding" announcing the door was ajar. After opening it a few inches, Hunter met some resistance. He repositioned himself and placed both legs against the jammed door, pushing. Metal creaked and cedar branches bent as the door opened further. Hunter leaned his shotgun against the truck and pulled himself free of the deer carcass. He felt the wet musk of deer blood on his face, but Hunter did have a sharp pain on his

God and Country

lip and chin. Gingerly, he placed his fingers to his face. That was going to need stitches; however, it would not affect him moving. But to where? Again, the same nagging question: "Now what?"

Food. That deer might be crushed, but it was still meat. How would he get the meat home? The truck was a wreck. There were no other vehicles. Hunter reckoned he was 5 miles from Grandma Tammy's house, and it would be getting dark soon. Was DHS going to send out other vehicles? Hunter went back to the truck and reached around to the back seat, found his hunting knife and a trash bag. He managed to pull the deer carcass out. In thirty minutes, Hunter had outed almost forty pounds of shoulders, quarters, and back straps and placed them in the bag. Hunter grabbed the bag, his shotgun, and prepared himself to cross-country back home. It wasn't his truck. Maybe DHS would never find out who was with Paul? No, they would see the deer carcass and know someone had made it out alive. There seemed to be no good answer.

Hunter made his way up the embankment to the road and took notice of the wreck. The abandoned semi trailer and the two wrecked military vehicles were somehow joined together. There was little left of the DHS agents in the first vehicle. Hunter automatically averted his eyes at the carnage. The second vehicle yielded less trauma, yet the same fatal effect. Two more dead. Well, Hunter would lose little sleep over those deaths tonight. He had been simply trying to find food for his family, and they probably would have killed him had they caught up with them.

Hunter's mind moved to pragmatism. Was there anything useful that he could sell? He looked at the first vehicle. He was not getting into that vehicle without a crane. Making his way back to the second M998. Inside the cab of the vehicle, secured within their rifle mounts, were two M4 assault rifles. Hunter eyed the rifles warily. Being caught with those rifles could mean his death. On the other hand, those rifles might fetch quite a hefty price from someone wanting to arm himself. Looking in the back, Hunter found an empty Army issue duffle bag. Making his decision, he took the two M4s and twelve 30 round magazines of 5.56 mm ball ammunition. As dusk fell, Hunter was headed across the fields of southwest Iowa, feeling like an early traveling Santa, with his Mossberg in hand and a 70 pound pack on his back.

"Now Hunter, I gotta tell ya." Grandpa Phil was talking with Hunter in the back room. "The deer is good, but ya damned near got yourself killed. What the hell good is food for your little girl in there if you are dead?"

Phil had an opinion on almost any topic of conversation. His round-about approach to verbal discourse was often augmented by a copious supply of alcohol. Holding to a bottle of conversational sustenance, Phil somehow always found a way of getting to the bottom line of a subject, and he did so then. "The bottom line is you can't win here in this town. Tammy and I will do just fine. We can go without, but this ain't no way to raise a little girl."

Hunter knew exactly what Phil was talking about. During the month that Hunter had been at Grandma Tammy's, the Department of Homeland Security had, in effect, taken over Clarinda, Iowa. The DHS was in the process of seizing corn silos throughout the region for "national security" reasons. This was a tall order, considering the amount of corn silos in the state of Iowa. Crops were still only half-harvested because of the diesel shortage, and although it was declared highly illegal, local townspeople had been driven by hunger to harvest dent corn by hand. In the fields south of the local airport, four men had been shot stealing what was deemed federal property. Since then, eight checkpoints had been set up around the town to reduce the chance of yet more "theft." Within a month following the so-called "Economic Meltdown," the correctional facility at the north edge of town had been abandoned. Rumors abounded. Some had it that prisoners had starved to death there. Other rumors held that Clarinda townsfolk were being detained and taken there now. Still others mentioned the federal government making plans to convert the facility into a mandatory boarding school, run by the Department of Agriculture, the FDA, and, of course, the Department of Homeland Security.

God and Country

"Well, damnit, Phil. There ain't no good choices here."

Phil simply nodded and took a silent sip. Finally, Phil spoke again. "Your brother Hank said basically the same thing. He is going to slip across the river and be here tonight. Said something about traveling down to Arkansas to be with your mom, Jason, and your little sis, Haley."

Hunter had seen Phil keeping in touch with the people in town, after he had closed up shop a month ago. Citizen band radio and handheld two-way radios were much in demand after cell service had ended. Phil had installed a CB radio in the shop out back, and the family managed to keep in contact with Hank by a handheld talkie stashed near the park and baseball complex. For the first week following the economy's collapse, the park had been somewhat busy. After that, fewer people traveled from their homes. There was simply little reason to leave them, except to wait in the food ration lines. The entire atmosphere of the town had changed. Hunter's older brother had apparently seen enough to know it was time to leave.

Hank was traveling light that evening. It had cooled off considerably, and there was a heavy frost on the field north of the local coop fertilizer company. The DHS checkpoint was nearby at Washington Street Bridge, but here, where Hank was to cross, the Nodaway River took a bend east, providing cover from unwanted observation. He made his way toward the river bank and undressed in the moonless night. He placed all of his clothes, his .45 automatic, ammunition, and a towel in a garbage bag, tying it tight. He then placed that garbage bag in another, leaving some air in the second one. Holding onto a small overhead branch, he walked down the dirt bluff into the depth of the meandering river, holding onto his improvised floatation device and kicking his feet. The water was cold, shocking Hank's core temperature as only his head and hands remained above the water. After about 50 feet crossing the gentle current, Hank's feet could feel the cold of a mucky bottom, and he moved his wooden legs, one in front of the other, until he made it to the shore. Chilled to the bone,

God and Country

Hank dried off in the cold Iowa night and dressed again. By midnight, Hank was at the back door of Grandma Tammy's place.

"I am not going," Brittany said petulantly.

"Brittany, they will take Hannah away," Hunter pleaded.

"I don't care. I will report you. We will freeze to death out there. There is no food; we will starve. For what? To go to Arkansas and find your mother?" There was a nasty sneer in her last statement. Continuing her sneer, she looked at Hunter. "You always screw things up."

"Are you crazy?" Hunter regretted the words as soon as they had passed his lips. "You don't care about the life of your daughter?" Hunter just shook his head and walked away. He needed a drink. Of course, that was just another thing that Brittany would be upset about.

Yet, after another 48 hours of screaming and accusations, Brittany grudgingly agreed to go with Hank and Hunter. Brittany had heard how the Department of Homeland Security had taken over Clarinda and abused their presumed authority. Hunter had held his ground, stating his daughter was going with him. It was left unsaid that Brittany was simply not welcome at Grandma's house without Hunter. The two brothers were loading up the SUV while the eight-year-old Hannah helped as much as she could. Brittany simply stood outside the vehicle with a cold stare and her arms crossed.

"It's going to be a long trip," Hunter thought as they finished packing.

Their trunk area was laden with food supplies. Backpacks had been prepared, carrying sleeping bags, tent material, and food supplies such as oatmeal, peanuts, and peanut butter. The SUV itself would contain heavier canned goods and blankets. The backpacks would travel next to each person. Even little Hannah had a backpack. "Grandma gave me a chocolate bar and some apple juice in mine," Hannah stated proudly.

Phil and Tammy gave their goodbye hugs to the crew. In doing so, Phil pulled two things from his coat pocket and gave them to Hunter. "I want you to have my pistol," Phil stated stiffly as he handed Hunter the long-barreled .357 Ruger. "It's a GP100. Holds seven shots. And, I don't need these shells either." He handed Hunter the box.

"Damnit, Phil. I can't take this. You love this thing."

"Oh, I ain't giving it to you. It is payment. You keep that great-granddaughter of ours safe."

Hunter started to protest further, but Phil said matter-of-factly, "You're keeping it, and that's the bottom line." Indeed it was.

Phil then went back to his truck, wiped some tears from his face, and retrieved something from under the seat. He walked up to Hank. "And you take this," handing Hank a familiar black-labeled bottle. "Share some with Hunter. Just some. You know how he gets." Phil and Hank laughed at the joke.

"Come back and see us, okay boys?" Grandma Tammy managed a smile, unable to stop the tears. Both Phil and Tammy realized they probably would never see them again. The SUV doors closed, the vehicle rolled down the driveway, and turned south toward an uncertain future.

—

It was a clear, starry night with only a crescent moon providing some light. Hunter's SUV moved forward slowly, with little light, so as to avoid attracting attention. The parking lights were turned on, but they had been taped up, so only a small covered slit of the parking light shone on the road. Hunter called that "blackout drive," something he had heard from one of his buddies in the Army. Hank worked navigation using a Rand McNally Road Atlas and a flashlight wrapped in red plastic gift wrap.

"Night vision," Hank explained.

Their traveling plans seemed sensible enough if they did not travel too fast, avoided the more traveled roads, drove on straighter roads that could be easily measured for distance, and otherwise avoided detection. Still, those were a lot of "ifs." The plan was to be well into Missouri by daybreak and hole up for the day.

Hunter checked his watch. They had been traveling for hours. Sunrise would be coming soon, and they needed to get the vehicle under good cover. The only problem was there seemed to be little cover along the roads. Having crossed the Missouri border around 1 a.m., the brothers had taken side roads, traveling south and east. They were trying to avoid all towns, but most roads led to towns. Now they found themselves traveling south on Highway 216 with what should be the town of Grant City about three miles ahead. The surrounding area was not wooded, and the brothers needed to find a safe hiding spot. A faint predawn glow to Hunter's left told him time was running out.

"Down there," Hank interrupted his thoughts. "That dark spot. Is that a pond?"

Hunter stopped the vehicle. The predawn light played tricks with his eyes. "Think so."

"A pond that big probably has a road running to it. I am going to get out and walk ahead," Hank announced. He did so, with an M4 in one hand and his "red lens" flashlight in the other.

Hank opened the door and got out of the passenger seat, and inside the vehicle grew cold, only partly due to the cool weather.

"Hell," Hunter thought, "Prison could not be any worse than being in here with her. Oh, yeah, Hank gets to leave?..." Hunter's internal monologue was the only respite from the hateful cold coming from someone he loved, or better said, had once loved.

What seemed like an eternity waiting for Hank, there was finally a knock at the window of the truck. It was Hank. He told what he had discovered. After walking about 200 feet, Hank had found a trail. "It's a road. Seems to be a wooded area and a pond up there a bit. I will lead you through."

Hank started walking ahead, the light of his red flashlight signaling them to move forward. Then, Hank turned off the road with the dark blue SUV directly behind him. Hank walked ahead, rifle at ready. Hunter had their windows down, feeling the cold chill of early dawn. The only sound was the steady rhythm of the engine breathing out through the tailpipe and the occasional crack of a twig or drop of a pebble. The wheel marks of the road were slowly becoming visible as the wooded area approached. As

God and Country

their vehicle entered the woods, Hunter smelled wood burning...and another familiar smell. Coffee.

Chapter 2

Congregation

"Can we help you?"

Hank turned to his right, an M4 carbine in hand.

"Unless you are trying to hurt someone, you don't have a need to point that gun at people."

In the growing light, an older gray bearded man with a sailing captain's hat came forward. Hunter put the vehicle in park, and stepped out. The two brothers walked off the path a couple of steps.

"Been a long night. You boys look like you could use a cup of coffee."

Brittany brought Hannah out, and they all walked toward an older RV in a clump of trees. The older gentleman picked up a metal percolator that had sat on a grate over the glowing embers. All of this seemed to give a perceivable warmth against the chill of the morning air.

"Are you the captain of a boat?" Hannah asked. The older man smiled broadly.

"What's your name?"

"Hannah," she said with a big smile on her face.

"Well, Hannah, no. Actually, I am a pastor of a church. Pastor John. I just always liked wearing this hat, and it didn't seem fitting to leave it behind."

"Where is your church?" Hannah asked innocently.

The older gentleman stood up and moved his hand throughout the woods. Among the trees, Hunter began to notice at least a dozen vehicles. Pickups, RVs, and cars were all inside the tree-line, well hidden among the pine and spruce trees of the forest.

"This is my church, or better said, God's church."

Hunter always had a problem with religion in general. Before, religious people had always struck him as a bunch of better-than-thou hypocrites. But this gentleman's easy, welcoming manner seemed to challenge Hunter's preconceived notions.

"Now I guess you know you are traveling during quite an interesting time," the pastor spoke to them around the fire. "You know what happened when the market collapsed, right? Money lost its value. Credit was closed. Electronic assets frozen. The trucks stopped carrying fuel and food…"

"We know that," Hunter interrupted. "But why did the Department of Homeland Security start bothering everyone? We ain't terrorists."

"The federal government is trying to hold onto power in a nation that cannot be fed," Pastor John continued patiently. "They are using our basic needs to 'keep us in line.' Food, supplies, anything of value is subject to federal confiscation. They say it is about national security. The way I see it, the only thing the President is trying to secure is another term in office, maybe an indefinite term." The pastor finished his coffee and up-ended it on a stick.

"My congregation and I are from Bethany, about 45 miles southeast of here. For some reason, DHS took an interest in our town. When the DHS attempted to mobilize the local National Guard units, it seems the Albany unit took issue with their role as 'security' when it involved forcing people from their homes. You know us stubborn Missourians. About that time, the people in our congregation decided it was time to leave before the shooting started. We have been here for two weeks now. Ya know, why don't you guys stay here with us? We sure could use you."

"We are headed to northeast Arkansas," Hunter replied.

"If you go south, you are bound for trouble. That is no place to take your wife and child."

"I hear what you are saying," Hank didn't speak much, but when he did, he had something worth saying. "We will go slow and be cautious. We'll stay off the roads if we have to, but we are headed to our mom's. If trouble finds us, we might give some back."

"Well then, stay till you decide to go," Pastor John smiled broadly in his reply. "You are welcome here."

God and Country

The family set up their sleeping bags in their vehicle. Brittany and Hannah slept in the back seat. Hunter remained in the front seat, sleep not coming to him easily. Slowly, he succumbed to a slumber.

Hank had agreed to take the first watch. And that was where he was now, with his bearded face, bare, bald head, and broad shoulders. Had it not been for the automatic assault rifle he was holding, he could have been mistaken for a Viking in the midst of that peaceful, pine forest.

About 15 minutes later, Vicky, John's wife, came up to him. "Want some breakfast?" The smell of fried potatoes and bacon had been making Hank's stomach tie itself in knots.

"Let me get the others up," Hank offered.

"Let 'em sleep. I will make another batch."

After breakfast, Hank walked the camp with Pastor John. There were about 40 people. Their intent was to wait it out here until things sorted themselves out a bit. Pastor John had been talking about the state of the country. "I mean, I love the U.S.A., but lately, it seems that this country has made some bad choices. When I spoke out to the local DHS commander about people being moved from their homes, I was told something about the necessity of "transportation security." He told me if I interfered with that security, he would arrest me...and my wife. So, I spoke with the congregation. For the most part, the church decided to leave."

At noon, the family awoke to a hearty meal of potatoes, eggs, and gravy. Hunter and his daughter ate together by the fire while Brittany stood apart, taking her breakfast by a group of trees.

"Momma's sad again," Hannah said to her dad.

"I know." Hunter did not want to address the obvious.

"Can you make her happy, Daddy?"

"I don't know. I just don't know."

After helping with the cleanup, Vicky and Brittany watched Hannah playing with ants crawling on the pine trees on that fine, autumn Missouri day. The older woman gleaned Brittany's mood, and conversation was sparse. The brothers, on the other hand, spoke readily with Pastor John about how they replenished their water supply, camp security, and the security situation around Missouri.

"I don't know much. Here-tell, St. Louis is a mess. A man came from there one week after this financial "meltdown" started. People were rioting in the streets. Not hearing much from Kansas City. Let's just hope we start hearing some good news."

Off in the distance came the sound of a very faint ratt, tatt, tatt. Both Hank and Hunter felt the irony of the moment. There. Another. Still far off.

"That's coming from Grant City. We left to escape all of that. We might have gone in the wrong direction." Pastor John's face showed concern.

As the day progressed, the automatic weapons fire had not stopped in the distance. In fact, it had become more sustained. At 3:30 pm, Pastor John met with everyone. They had determined it was best to move northwest.

"I know this isn't my meeting and all, but it ain't any better where we came from. Just saying," Hunter interjected into the meeting.

"So where should we go?" one man asked Hunter, pleadingly.

Hunter had no answer.

Pastor John spoke up. "We go somewhere where we don't hear that."

Within 45 minutes, the caravan was packed up and ready to go.

"We can go with them. They can help protect us. They have guns, too," Brittany said, knowing her husband and brother-in-law would not agree.

"They are going in the wrong direction. Back toward Iowa," Hank responded.

Of course, Brittany realized this, but that didn't seem to matter. "I am going with them. And, I am taking my daughter."

When Hunter did not reply, Hank did. "To hell you will."

Brittany, unsure of the decision herself, relented, yet almost cried when Pastor John and Vicky pulled away, leading the caravan up the trail to the road. Hank walked behind the caravan until it cleared the woods, then watched it as it made its way the quarter mile of the trail to the road. The trail of vehicles slowly turned right, heading north. The caravan was not quite out of sight behind a bend in the woods when the last two visible vehicles stopped.

Hunter walked over to Hank and the two brothers watched in silence. Someone on the road was talking, but it was hard to make out. Then other voices raised. Someone was yelling. A young man and woman quietly left a green minivan with their two children. They were making their way down the gentle embankment to the field below. "Stop!" someone shouted. Two soldiers carrying rifles rounded the front of the minivan, followed by another. The third soldier, apparently in charge, unholstered his pistol, took aim, and shot the young father in the back. The young woman ran to her husband, screaming hysterically. The officer again leveled his pistol at the field below and shot her twice. He then muttered to the two soldiers and walked away. One soldier raised the rifle and quickly dispatched the little blonde-haired girl. The other soldier was having difficulty hitting his target, a ten-year old boy. His colleague placed his hand on the other's raised rifle, staying him. Then he raised his own, aimed carefully, and brought the boy down with a three-round burst. The other soldier appeared to congratulate him, patting him on the back.

Hank couldn't believe what he had just seen. As the events realized themselves in his mind, so did a livid fury. He raised his M4, sighted in on one of the soldiers that had just murdered two children. He would have fired had it not been for Hunter, who grabbed his face with both hands. "Stop," Hunter shouted in a whisper. He pointed to Hannah.

Brittany had also watched the scene in disbelief. She said nothing, yet understood that, had Hank not stopped her, both she and her daughter could have been killed as that family had been. Only after Hannah, who had heard the shooting, came up beside her mother and touched her hand, did Brittany react to the barbarous scene by starting to cry, first slowly, then uncontrollably. Hunter walked over to his wife, instinctively wanting to comfort her. He stiffly placed his arm around her and held her.

"They are still up there," Hank announced as he walked back to the vehicle.

"It has been an hour. What are they waiting on?" Hunter questioned.

"Transportation? I think they are waiting on larger vehicles to take the church people."

"You mean Pastor John's congregation." These were the first words Brittany had spoken since witnessing the horrific event.

"We can't let this happen," Hunter stated plainly.

"It has already happened," Hank responded. "There is a mother and father lying dead in that field with their two children."

"We gotta do something."

"Hunter, look at your daughter. Look at Hannah! That dead little girl is the same age as Hannah. Get it?"

"Which is why we gotta do something, Hank. We can't let that stand."

It was obvious to Hank that his brother was right. Hunter's family, if indeed he could call it that, had to be protected, but it was wrong to let those murders go unanswered. It was wrong to abandon Pastor John.

Hank finally nodded his head. "I know," he said.

"Okay, Brittany, you will stay with Hannah here. That part is non-negotiable. If Hank and I don't come back in two hours, I want you to take your backpacks and make your way back to Iowa. Walk, don't drive. It should only take you about a day." Hunter gave his wife the .357 and a quick kiss. He scooped Hannah up and hugged her tight.

Hank and Hunter left the girls. Skirting along a fence line toward the road, they paused as they approached the road.

"Okay, let's assume they don't have extra transportation," Hank whispered, "...and they haven't sent down extra soldiers to scout the area. I think they might not have a lot of people with them."

"What's the plan?" Hunter asked.

"Let's look around."

God and Country

Doing a quick recon, the brothers noticed seven men wearing DHS uniforms. Six of them were armed with M4 assault rifles. The soldier with the pistol, who had murdered the family, seemed to be in charge. Four soldiers were guarding Pastor John's congregation. They appeared to be simply waiting, smoking cigarettes, and not worried about security. There were two hummers which had been blocking the pastor's convoy. One hummer had an M240 machine gun mounted atop. For some reason, however, it was not manned.

Hank laid out a plan, then left his brother. Hunter was to position himself below the convoy toward the rear of the formation. Hank was to cross the road and make his way along the crest of the ridge, following the road to the front of the convoy.

Below the road, Hunter high-crawled into a firing position in a group of bushes near the embankment. Surprise was of the essence. Would there be innocent people killed? Most likely. But, having witnessed firsthand the inhumane actions of the DHS, it was better to risk casualties.

From the top of the small ridge, Hank watched the scene below. The officer with the pistol was talking to Pastor John, who was on his knees. The pastor was bloodied in the face, obviously roughed up from a previous encounter. The officer asked the pastor something, yelled, then went over and grabbed his wife Vicky by the hair. He held his pistol to her head.

A shot exploded a split second before the officer's head did. Hank cycled the hunting rifle quickly, pulling the trigger again. A second soldier went down. Hank missed a third, as the soldier made his way behind the caravan of vehicles. He put down the hunting rifle and picked up the M4.

Hunter waited until Hank began their assault. The soldier who had escaped Hank's deadly fire was not able to escape Hank's younger brother. Hunter shot the escaping soldier in the chest as he rounded the vehicles. The guards were abandoning their prisoners, running for cover offered by the hummers. For the most part, the congregation were staying down, trying to avoid the gun battle going on around them.

God and Country

Hank and Hunter had three of the soldiers pinned down behind the right side of the caravan, but one soldier had managed to make his way to the cover of the two hummers. Pastor John got up, grabbed the rifle from a dead soldier, and ran toward the hummers, firing as he ran. The DHS soldier behind the hummer was getting in the turret. He pulled up his M4 and shot the pastor. Pastor John went down. The DHS soldier then charged the M240 machine gun and began spraying the hill where Hank was positioned. Bullets, rocks, and dust exploded all around Hank.

The gunner then traversed and began firing at Hunter's position. Hunter was pinned down. Suddenly, the machine gun stopped. Pastor John, still lying in a puddle of his own blood, had managed to fire off a three-round burst at the machine gunner. The DHS agent hung loosely over the turret atop the hummer, shot dead. The sudden silence stunned the three remaining soldiers, and they came slowly out with their hands up. Hunter came running up behind them as Hank quickly walked down the hill, weapon trained.

The congregation began getting up. One man gathered the weapons from the DHS soldiers. Vicky had run to her husband and was talking with him. Hank walked over. Pastor John managed a smile at Hank, blood in his teeth. "I will pray for you and your family." The pastor fought for another breath, then stopped fighting.

—

The three soldiers were secured by the congregation members, tied with the same plastic zip ties they themselves had used on the congregation members. The dead bodies were stripped of weapons, then thrown in the field below. The two hummers, four of the assault rifles, and the M240 machine gun were taken as well.

"What will you do? Where will you go?" Hunter asked the pastor's wife.

The congregation had experienced a severe blow, but Vicky, the dead pastor's wife, was holding up remarkably well.

"We will do as John said. We will go where we do not hear that deadly noise again."

"But north is just as bad."

Vicky placed her hand on Hunter's shoulder. Her sad voice took on a prognostic tone. "We both have our paths. But, sometimes you have to travel *through* the storm before you can see the right way to go." Her eyes held tears. Her expression was both dark and resolute. As if in response to Vicky's words, the darkening north Missouri sky began a light drizzle. Vicky got into the Winnebago, put the vehicle in drive, and the convoy rolled away.

Chapter 3

Loss

The brothers left in the other direction, through the darkening field, to the woods where Brittany and Hannah awaited. They were carrying two extra assault rifles, two ammo cans of 5.56 mm ball ammunition, and extra magazines as well.

"We cannot take the SUV. It is too dangerous. We need to go on foot and go now."

Hank had studied the map enough to realize he needed a better map if they were going to be traveling on foot. Until he could find something better, they would need to stick to traveling right off the roads.

The four had just moved out when headlights lit up the road a half mile distant. "Keep moving, say nothing, they won't see us out here," Hank whispered.

The vehicle stopped on the road and shone a spotlight across the field just as the last of the four were entering the forest opposite the pond. No danger for the moment. The light drizzle changed to a more heavy rain. No time to stop; they had to keep moving away from the danger. Hunter kept thinking of the violence of the past two hours. Of Pastor John in the puddle of blood, of the little blonde-haired girl falling......keep moving.

And that's what they did for the next hour. Hank and Hunter kept pace, with Brittany and Hannah following them. Hannah was quite mature for being eight years old. She understood the gravity of the situation, and took the weary, wet travel in stride the best she could. After they crossed a road, Hank stopped in the tree line.

"That should be Highway 256," Hank commented. "I just can't tell anymore because of...this." Hank was holding no longer a book, but a wilted mess of pages sticking together, starting to fall apart. "We need to find some cover from this rain and dry off somehow," Hank muttered.

After a while of traveling cross country alongside the highway, they found an old cow barn. There was no house nearby and the stalls were all empty. There was, however, dry straw. Although the backpacks were waterproof, their clothing was not. The ponchos had succeeded in keeping their upper bodies somewhat dry, but their pants and boots were soaked. The family stripped off their pants, found their dry poncho liners, and began to make beds in the straw.

    Hunter looked through the backpack he had prepared. The backpacks had been packed light, and provided calories to keep the family moving. Each backpack contained instant potatoes, instant oatmeal, coffee, sugar, rice, flour, and salt. An old coffee camping percolator was in Hunter's bag, if for nothing else, simply to boil water. Come to find out, Grandma Tammy had packed a chocolate bar for not only Hannah, but for each of them. Besides the ponchos and liners, the backpacks contained tin cups, two mess kits, matches, spare socks, ski hats, work gloves, hunting knives, filled plastic water bottles and iodine...and a med kit with extra ibuprofen. Hunter had gone through most of his bag before he found what he needed. A dry pair of boxers. "Thank God," Hunter thought.

    Hunter's mind wandered to what all he had left behind. He thought of Phil and Tammy, and hoped they would be okay. He still had Phil's .357 and remembered the promise he had made. Hunter would miss his Mossberg shotgun, but the M4 was a more effective weapon, its ammunition lighter. He had left it behind along with the extra canned food in the car. There was simply no way to carry all that extra weight.

    Hunter had had some problems sleeping during the night, not from the cold, but from what he had seen. People shouldn't kill people. That was wrong. Not from some stupid, religious point-of-view. Hell, no. It was wrong because that was another person. The officer had shot that man and woman. The soldiers who had shot those children. They were evil. But, hadn't he himself done the same thing? Another soldier he had killed had not murdered anyone. Had that really been necessary? He tried to brush off the thoughts from his mind, but they seemed to linger, even in his sleep. Hunter had dreamt that he was an executioner, lining up people and shooting them in the back of the head. Each would fall face forward into

God and Country

the dirt. The last person in the execution line was a small, blonde-haired girl. She looked up. It was Hannah. The shock startled Hunter awake.

—

After a talk with Hank, Hunter set out to scout the outskirts of Grant City. Although the rain had stopped, it had grown colder during the night, and the temperature felt a few degrees above freezing this morning. "About 37 degrees maybe," Hunter thought.

The town looked dead. No one would suspect a person going for a stroll, right? He turned on what was 2nd Street, passing a local convenience store that had been abandoned. None of their famous pepperoni pizza there anymore, Hunter thought to himself, his stomach growling at the disappointing thought. Its windows were broken, and the gas nozzles actually cut from the pumps. But down further, past a boarded-up supermarket, there was smoke.

Hunter continued forward. He had his .357 under his green military issue field jacket, and he felt it reassuringly. He saw a Humvee ahead. It was parked in front of the Worth County Courthouse. Next to the court house was what remained of the post office. Some huge explosion had apparently blasted through the brick building. A haze of smoke lingered low to the ground along with the smell of gunpowder.

As Hunter walked around the hummer, he saw someone sitting up against the passenger door of the military vehicle. In his lap was a M4 without any magazine. The soldier was softly weeping.

"Hey, are you okay, man?" Hunter came up to the man. Wrong choice of words. The soldier, a Sergeant Panning, simply shook his head.

"My sons. Both of them. Dead. First my wife. Now them."

As the soldier spoke, Hunter learned that Staff Sergeant Panning was a member of the 2/104, a National Guard Field Artillery detachment out of Albany, Missouri. When DHS had tried to pressure their unit into helping with relocation operations, most of the unit resisted.

"We simply drove off in our hummers with what we had. Went back to Albany. They attacked our Guard Center with M2 Bradleys that came down from Iowa. We didn't stand a chance. My two sons were with me there. Tyler was killed while we were drawing weapons. Then they chased us here. This is my little boy, Jordan." He hugged the neck of the young soldier laying in his lap.

"What kind of sick joke is this?" Panning looked up at Hunter with pain in his eyes. "I risked my life in Iraq for this country, and now our country hunts my family down like animals?"

"They may be coming back."

"I don't care. I have nothing to live for."

"You are from here, right?"

"So?"

"You can help us find our way."

"There is only one way for me now."

"I have a wife, a little girl, and my brother. We are trying to get to our mom in Arkansas."

Silence.

"Please."

A few minutes later, the two men were walking together. Two blocks away was another hummer, burned out, its sides riddled with large caliber holes. Three soldiers inside were also burned beyond recognition. Coming back, on the other side of the courthouse, was an M939 five-ton vehicle with communications shelter mounted on the back. It had been abandoned with the doors open.

"I think this is what we need." SSG Panning pivoted himself atop the back of the truck to the large sand-colored box and opened the door of the communications shelter. A few minutes later, Panning returned with an old military-issue satchel containing what looked like plastic covered maps inside. In his other hand, he had a lensatic compass.

"Now, I just need to get a couple more things." Rounding the courthouse, they returned to SSG Panning's humvee. He opened the rear cargo door, wildly rooting through the crowded cargo bed, exclaiming "Where is it?" and throwing the occasional ammo magazine or MRE out the back.

God and Country

"There you are, my baby!" Panning sounded emotional, irrational. He backed from the rear of the hummer with something in his hands. The sergeant squatted on the asphalt, embracing an olive-drab canvas bag as if it were a child. He gently opened the bag's cover, reached inside, then looked up at Hunter and spoke. "They murdered my family," the man stated matter-of factly with a slight smile, but dead serious eyes. "Now, I swear to God, there will be payback." It was only then that Hunter noticed the curved rectangle that Panning was holding. Three words were embossed on its surface, bringing a chill down Hunter's spine: "FRONT TOWARD ENEMY."

That afternoon Hunter and SSG Panning made their way back to the barn. Hank was drying clothes in the afternoon sun. Brittany was cooking oatmeal over a small stick fire.

"Well, at least she is helping out," Hunter thought.

As if his wife had heard him, Brittany looked from the mess kit. She didn't quite smile, but at least it wasn't a scowl.

Hunter introduced SSG Panning to the family. The sergeant nodded, sat in front of the fire, not saying much, and distantly gazing into the flame.

Hank took Hunter aside. "Something about this guy isn't right."

Hunter countered, "He lost his wife. Dunno how. But he just lost both of his sons today. Give him a break."

"I just don't think Panning needs to have any ammunition for that gun of his, at least not for now."

"He doesn't need any. He is just here to point the way."

That evening the family moved out, with somewhat dry clothes. The clear night boasted a bright, waxing crescent moon that had risen about 10 p.m. They made good time, being able to walk along the untraveled roads. SSG Panning was in the lead, walking ahead, alone. Hank walked behind him with the others. Every once in a while, he would follow along with the map. Hank noticed that the lettered roads were less traveled than the numbered system. He walked up to SSG Panning and asked about it.

God and Country

"Those are county roads," SSG Panning gave his one sentence reply. Hank wondered why SSG Panning never had given his first name. As Panning continued, Hank waited for the others. Something was not right.

Nevertheless, the family had made good time that night, finding themselves at a brown and yellow road sign announcing they had arrived at "Grant Trace State Forest." They set up camp under a forest mostly denuded of the colorful leaves that made Missouri October's so beautiful. No need for tents, they decided. Instead, they simply pulled out their sleeping bags. Hunter lay awake, admiring the stars, which were magnificent now that the moon had set. Beside him, his daughter slept soundly. On the other side of his daughter, Hunter's wife lay awake, staring at the same stars. She did not look at Hunter, nothing was said, but Hunter felt there was some hope for his marriage after all.

Later, as the family slept, the predawn began to color the sky with reds and oranges, casting a magic spell on the forest.

Brittany stirred awake, quietly unzipped the bag, and tried her best not to disturb Hannah, who was a hot mess of sleep snuggled next to her. Hannah stirred as Brittany got up, but then she rolled over to her dad, muttering "Momma." Brittany left quietly to find a place to relieve herself, while also trying to find a quiet place to think.

Later, Hunter awoke to the morning sun. He reached over to place his hand over to his daughter. Hannah groaned. Brittany, however, was not there. Up already? Hunter got up.

"Hank, where is Brittany?"

"Huh?" Hank had been sound asleep.

SSG Panning was keeping watch, sitting up against an almost empty maple tree, staring at the fire.

"Panning, have you seen Brittany?" Hunter asked the sergeant.

Nothing. A maple seed twirled down in front of the sergeant's face. Hunter noticed the sergeant's eyes, tormented by invisible demons.

"Panning!"

"Huh? What?"

"Have you seen Brittany?"

The sergeant shook his head, his eyes haunted.

A vehicle was starting in the distance. Hunter ran to the top of the hill and saw a hummer to the east about 150 yards away parked in a gravel parking lot next to a paved road. A uniformed man was putting someone in the vehicle. It was Brittany. The hummer turned as it drove away. On the passenger door was a marking Hunter was very familiar with, a blue emblem of a war eagle clutching a shield: Homeland Security.

Hunter stared in disbelief as the hummer pulled away toward town, then came to his senses and ran back down the hill. He woke up his brother.   "Brittany! They took her!"

"Who?"

"Homeland."

Although Hank and Hunter did not notice, SSG Panning's attention had finally been captured.

"Hannah." Hunter stirred his daughter. He picked her up and carried her to a nearby trailhead. He opened up the side door of a green, rectangular container labeled "Trash--Recycle" and pulled out a plastic garbage bag, throwing it behind a group of trees. "I want you to hide in here. Go back to sleep. I will be back for you no matter what….wait here."

Hannah nodded. "What do you want me to do again?"

"Go back to sleep. Wait here. Mommy and I will be back for you soon," Hunter felt a knife in his gut as he said the words. Still, it was better that Hannah did not know.

Backpacks were hidden; the men were traveling light. M4s, pistols, extra magazines stuffed in their jackets, hunting knives. Where would they find her? Their best guess was back in town.

As they moved, Hank began to reflect. Both Hunter and SSG Panning seemed too distraught to think, but Hank realized they had no "plan" except to get Brittany. That was not a plan. They needed a way to get in close without being noticed. There would be guards. How many? Were they simply going to their deaths trying to rescue his brother's wife?

As they approached the small town's residential area, Hank stopped SSG Panning. Hunter was wondering why Hank had stopped him.

"Look," Hank spoke to the two others behind the water-stained side of a white utility shed. "We need to get a layout of the place. Let's stop, get information, and make a plan. Otherwise, they will simply capture us, too." As Hank spoke, a Humvee drove slowly past the small building. Although the patrol had not seen them, the event lent more credence to Hank's words. "And, I think I have an idea that will get us in closer."

Two DHS agents were driving their patrol vehicle back into town. Ahead of them was something in the road. A person. Apparently, the person had been carrying firewood and had collapsed. At first, the driver thought he would simply drive over him. "Damned locals." Then he noticed the untrimmed brush might catch under his vehicle, or worse, the body. There would be hell to pay if he damaged the hummer. Slowly, the driver brought his hummer to a stop. His partner, wary of the situation, dismounted the vehicle. He scanned the vehicle's flank, then walked forward, a helmeted menacing figure in Level 4 body armor, his assault rifle trained on the body ahead. The DHS agent first pushed the body with the muzzle of his assault rifle, then knelt to turn it over. The agent was careful to turn the body away from him to guard against explosions. The face of the body was covered with blood.

"Country hick," the agent thought. Then the body opened its eyes. The last thing to go through that unfortunate DHS agent's mind was a .357 Magnum hollow-point. At point blank range, the large caliber pistol round entered through the agent's chin, passing through his sinuses, and out the top of his skull. The round hit the inside of the agent's kevlar. Although the lead projectile did not penetrate the laminate armor, it did propel the helmet, causing it to jump off the remnants of the dead agent's head, snapping the helmet strap off the destroyed chin. The noise of the explosion was deafening.

God and Country

The shot was a signal for both Hank and SSG Panning to pop up from camouflaged positions at the edge of the road. The driver put his vehicle in gear as Hank ran in front of the driver's windshield while Panning approached from the side, both with weapons raised. The driver stopped the vehicle and put his hands up.

Fifteen minutes later, the driver still had his hands up, having had them pulled over his head with a stretch of WD1 field wire. The driver also had the front of his shirt cut open. Three rather wicked-looking gashes were over his lower torso.

Through a brutal interrogation, Hank had found out that Brittany was at the Harrison County Courthouse. A little more "probing" revealed that there were three guards at the perimeter gate. Machine guns were at two corners of the courthouse, potentially covering all avenues of approach.

"Why is she at the courthouse? She didn't do anything wrong?"

"The tent," the tortured agent breathed out. "In the tent."

"What tent...why?"

"For the men."

"Fucking bastards!" Hunter breathed through gritted teeth. A second shot from the .357 rang out.

Hank climbed the fire escape behind a two-story bank building to recon the county courthouse. From the corner of the second floor roof, he noticed a big tent there. Climbing back down, he briefed Hunter and Panning. Hunter could barely contain his fury. Panning sat quietly, patiently listening. They would drive the hummer to the perimeter gate and hopefully get through quietly. Hank and SSG Panning were wearing the uniforms and helmets of the two dead agents. SSG Panning was to ride in the back with Hunter, who was to be their prisoner.

Hank felt a tense knot build in his stomach as he approached the gate. This was still suicide. What were the odds of rescuing Brittany? Yet, what choice did they have? He pulled up to the checkpoint; the guard signaled stop and approached the window. Then the guard appeared distracted by a sound, no, a scream. A woman's scream amidst the sound of a crowd whistling, laughing, and catcalling.

"You don't wanna miss today's entertainment," the guard smiled knowingly. "Got a real looker."

Hunter's anger rose within him, yet he restrained himself as the guard waved them through.

—

Driving ahead, Hank heard a thud, then another behind him. He turned around to find his brother Hunter unconscious. SSG Panning had Hunter's M4 trained on Hank.

"I'm sorry. You can't save her, and I have to do this." Panning stated without expression, a dead look in his eyes. "But," the sergeant continued, "those bastards will pay for my family…for our families." Hank watched helplessly as Panning dismounted the vehicle and ran toward the tent. SSG Panning threw down the assault rifle. As the sergeant moved toward the canvas door, Hank could make out what looked to be a trigger. In fact, it was an M57 igniting device. When SSG Panning entered the GP medium canvas tent, the M57 delivered an electric signal to a blasting cap mounted atop an M18 Claymore mine. The blasting cap detonated 1.5 pounds of C4 explosive, sending 700 metal ball bearings into the tent at a 60 degree angle. Within a millisecond, the tent looked to take a breath. Then, the top of the tent lifted high while still managing to contain the explosion, which sounded like a platoon of riflemen firing downrange in unison. The sides and back of the tent, as well as anyone within it, was penetrated by hundreds of small steel ball bearings. The tent canopy then burst into flames, receiving the heat shock of the explosion.

"No!!!" Hank was unable to hear himself scream after the ear-deadening explosion.

The guards from the shack were running toward the remnants of the tent and just stood there, dumbfounded. A siren started to sound as Hank watched the remaining canvas rest over the dead souls inside. Then, a clanging. A guard was firing at the hummer. Hank placed the vehicle in drive, spinning grass as he turned the accelerating vehicle, and crashed through the guard shack, spider-webbing the passenger windshield of the reinforced glass.

Hank made speed, turning left on Taylor Street, flying as fast as the governor-controlled throttle would allow, as he took the right curve of Highway W back toward the state park.

A few minutes later, the military vehicle was pulled to the side of the road.

Hunter had just awoke. Hank told him, in the most gentle way possible, what had happened. Was there a gentle way? Hunter could not comprehend his brother at first, then incomprehension was replaced by grief and rage.

"Go back," Hunter yelled in tears.

"I am so sorry, brother. But, we can't."

Confused, Hunter drew his pistol, pointing the .357 at his brother's head.

"Damn it. I said "Go back!"

"You need to be there for your daughter now. Killing yourself or me isn't an option," Hank explained as tears were streaming down his own face.

"Hannah," Hunter murmured, his shaky voice barely able to make a sound. The sound brought a second of mild relief to Hunter's tortured face. Hunter slowly lowered the .357 and broke down, sobbing again, uncontrollably.

Hank held his brother, catching breaths between his own bouts of sorrow. "I know it hurts," Hank uttered as he pulled his weeping brother's head to his chest. "I've been there, too."

Two hours later, Hunter had composed himself enough to return for his daughter. "Momma had to go away, Hannah."

"Dad, go away where?"

"Momma went to heaven."

"Dad, I ain't a kid anymore. You mean she died?"

Hunter nodded.

God and Country

"She..." Hannah began to swallow, her breathing became ragged. The father and daughter held each other. It was all they could do. All they had. They both felt helpless. Hannah felt the deep, empty hurt of missing her mother, while Hunter discovered that, despite all the cruel pain his wife had caused him, he had still loved her.

For the next two days, the three travelers did not move. They recovered from a shock of a hurt that wasn't going away. But time has a way of moving on even when you want to stay put. And such it was with Hank, Hunter, and Hannah.

—

"Daddy, I am hungry," Hannah said at last.

Hunter ran his finger through his girl's hair, reminding him of someone else. "Just like her ....No. Not doing that." He began the simple chore of building a stick fire, and heating up the instant oatmeal, adding plenty of sugar. It is strange how physical circumstances can intertwine and interfere with the emotions of one's mind. In this case, hunger and sorrow were permanently associated together where, for years afterward, Hannah would weep gently whenever she felt hungry, not knowing why. Also, for the rest of Hannah's life, eating oatmeal would bring with it certain sorrow.

That afternoon, the family prepared to leave Grant Trace Forest. Hunter had the duty of unpacking his wife's backpack. The extra food was a necessity. The extra poncho and liner were taken as well. Everything else was abandoned. Hannah said she wanted to carry her mother's assault rifle. Hunter said it was too dangerous, and it would make her a target. Hannah said she was almost nine, and she could help more. Hank quietly pointed out that Brittany was not armed when she had been abducted. He said he could help carry the rifle if needed. Hunter was already carrying an extra M4, but he saw the value of extra weapons. Besides, it did keep Hannah quiet. And so the three left. It was dusk, and only one week into their journey, yet it seemed like an eternity since they had left the relatively quiet town of Clarinda.

God and Country

Hunter's loss and confusion weighed on his mind, but that night's traveling itself proved uneventful. Walking down the less traveled roads of backcountry Missouri was convenient. Any vehicle approaching would usually be seen well in advance, and the family would simply ditch to the side of the road before anyone could see them. One good thing about the maps that SSG Panning had located for them was the detail. It allowed Hank to locate water sources. In this case, it showed a place off of Highway Y that provided both cover and a good water source: a very large pond.

"Of course, that pond water would need to be strained, boiled, and purified with iodine first. No need to get the runs on the run," Hank quipped silently.

Walking fast, the family made camp, filled water bottles, and slept. As they were preparing oatmeal, they saw smoke in the distance.

Chapter 4

Oppression

"That should be the town of Chillicothe. Doesn't look good," Hank wrinkled his forehead.

"Can we go around it?"

"We have to cross the river." Hank responded. "Going another way will cost us sixty miles. We have about a mile after the bridge before we get to town. My plan is to turn south here and go across, bypassing the town almost completely."

"Is that a church?"

"Yup. We will go right by there."

That night, it only took an hour to make the bridge. Hank was cautious. Although it was a small river, there was no way he wanted to get wet by fording it, especially with an eight-year-old. They would have to chance crossing the bridge if they could. Walking up the dirt bank of the bridge, Hank watched and waited, then upon seeing no sign of any sentries, Hank cleared the guard rail and ran a zig-zag pattern across the bridge. Hank hit the other guard rail with his rifle, signaling all clear. Hunter cleared the metal rail, then swung his daughter over it. They both ran across the bridge to Hank.

"Where to?" Hunter asked his brother.

As soon as Hunter spoke the words, the family saw headlights swing into view about a mile away. Jumping the guardrail, they ran down the embankment, past a small clearing, and into the woods below.

"Daddy, what is that bad smell?" Hannah asked as the three made their way through a maze of birch saplings.

Up ahead, the woods opened more into a clearing with a building off in the distance. A slight fog hung in the air, and with the fog the unmistakable stench of death. As the family cleared the woods, they noticed the yellow warning tape wrapped somewhat haphazardly around the building itself. "Caution--Do not enter" the tape warned. Where

God and Country

Hunter stayed back with his daughter, the older brother walked carefully up to the front entrance of the brick building. The smell was overpowering. Hank began to retch as he tried the door. Locked. There must be another entrance. He walked around to the back of the brick building. Like most small churches, the windows were small and high, perhaps to make the building more energy efficient, perhaps to discourage a break-in, something Hank was attempting to do right now. The white metal back door had rust spots at its bottom, but nevertheless seemed quite solid. Hank checked it. Locked up. Hank kicked at the door. There was no give. He then walked around to the side of the building. The air conditioning unit. Hank had worked HVAC in the past. He had installed this very unit several times for businesses in Council Bluffs. Which is how Hank noticed something that should not be there: the small flex hose mounted in the top of the main air duct. Hank recognized the galvanized steel exhaust hose. Facts added up in Hank's mind, and the results hit his mind at the same time the putrid smell of death, yet again hit his olfactory senses with a vengeance. This time, nothing could stop Hank from hitting his knees, vomiting, and continuing to retch and gag after the meager contents of his belly had been purged.

 Hank got to his feet, moved away from the building, and rather unsteadily made his way back to the edge of the parking lot, where Hunter and Hannah had been concealed behind the cover of a large oak tree.

 "What did you see?" Hunter asked.

 "Later. Let's move on."

 Hank studied the map, with his imagination still haunting what he had seen. There was no mistaking that the church had been the site of a mass execution. That the federal government could do such a thing seemed impossible. Yet Hank had witnessed what they had done with Brittany. Hank tried to shake it off, but both he and Hunter felt in their bones that there was a reckoning needed, a debt to be paid.

 "If we go to the end of this gravel road then keep walking that same direction, we should run into the end of a county road in about a kilometer." Hank gave direction in meters, as did the military map he was using. "That is a bit more than half a mile. There should be no traffic. Here, however," Hank placed his finger into the red glow of the flashlight, "we have another river crossing. The bridge looks longer. Could be dangerous, but there doesn't seem to be another way."

The light of the late rising moon created an eerie glow through the fog. Hank looked down at the luminous dial of his lensatic compass. He was no expert at reading it, but was learning. For now, Hank simply kept the dial turned to the azimuth as he walked following the glow. Although Hank was familiar with the concept of a pace count, he had no idea how many of his own steps were 100 meters. He guessed 130 steps. He realized he needed more practice at this. After traveling what he had estimated over 1200 meters, Hank realized that his attempt to navigate in the dark had fallen short of success. The fog had thickened, and the three felt they were traveling blind. No, not exactly blind. They were between a country road and the river, traveling toward Highway 36, which should be about another mile ahead.

The ground began to give under their feet, becoming mushy. The three were forced to travel more to their left. And then, a chain link fence.

"Ruuh, ruuh, ruur, ruur, ruff!" came what sounded like a smaller dog. "Ruur, ruff!"

"Who's there?" An older man came out, holding a small light in his hand. The dog continued to bark. "Come out, or I will call Homeland."

Hank emerged holding his M4 at ready. "Look, we don't want any trouble."

"We don't have any food. We don't have anything," the old man pleaded. "They took it all," the man muttered with a lower voice.

"We won't take anything from you," Hannah spoke up, walking up to the fence to pet the beagle. Hannah looked up at the old man. "We have food," she offered innocently. "Are you hungry?"

Inside the house, the man led the three to the kitchen. The room was dimly lit with two candles.

"Martha, we have guests."

God and Country

Hunter pulled out a two-liter soda bottle filled with rice. "We haven't eaten all day. Can we cook food here?"

"Do you know how much that is worth?" the older man asked. "Rice?"

"Not much food around here."

Hunter looked at the old man and his wife. For the first time, he noticed a certain hollowness to the older couple's cheeks, the look brought about by hunger. "Gotta place to cook?" Hunter asked.

The older woman directed him to the fireplace. Soon, the iron dutch oven hanging over the fire was filled with steaming cooked rice. Where Hunter, Hank, and Hannah ate heartily, the older couple were obviously ravenous, and kept apologizing as they gulped bite after bite.

"You need to slow down. You might get sick."

The man paused first, then his wife.

"I am so sorry," the elderly man said. "We haven't introduced ourselves properly. I am Melvin Painter, and this is my wife, Martha."

A conversation ensued about the events that had occurred in the last two months. It was mostly a one-sided conversation, as the two brothers did not want to talk about what had happened that week.

"How did you get here?" Melvin asked

"We took the north bridge, then went through the woods," Hunter offered.

"That makes sense. It is the only bridge that is not guarded. DHS keeps the checkpoint back toward town...because of the smell."

"Yeah, what was that smell? It was horrible," Hannah said, unaware of the subject she was broaching.

Not answering the little girl directly, Melvin turned to her and stated sadly, "Some people are not very nice." Then, without being able to contain himself, he continued. "Some people are evil." The old man held back tears.

Recovering, Melvin continued. He explained that he and Martha had a daughter. Now DHS had her.

God and Country

"That is why we get to live out here. I worked the power grid in town for twenty-eight years. The last ten years, I worked alongside my daughter's husband, Robert. I taught him everything he knows about the electric grid, and I know a lot. Without that knowledge, that dam won't keep producing electricity. When DHS were resettling the town, they needed Robert and me to keep the lights on. They let Martha and me stay put here out of town. Mighty big of 'em." The bitterness in Melvin's voice was evident. "They just took Angie, our daughter… 'to keep her safe' they said."

When they got done eating, the brothers made a gift of the container of rice and another plastic container of oatmeal for the older couple. Then, they prepared to leave. Hannah looked up at Hunter: "But, Dad."

"Later, kid." Hunter stated. They left out the back door and walked to the back yard's fence.

"Ya know, we have to cross the river and that patrol is right at the bridge," Hank had already begun to think about the route ahead.

"Uncle Hank, we can't leave!" Hannah stated emphatically.

"Huh?" Hank muttered as if puzzled, but he knew what his young niece was talking about.

"We have to help them! We can't just leave like this. Those people have their daughter. Those are the people that killed Momma, right?"

Hank looked at Hunter, then nodded. They both wanted to keep the narrative simple. The truth is there was enough blame in Brittany's death to go around. Hunter had unwittingly trusted someone who should not have been trusted. Hank had simply watched as the troubled sergeant played the role of a vengeful suicide bomber. He could, however, keep Brittany's death simple for her daughter, letting her think only the "bad guys" were to blame. Hank and Hunter, however, both felt a heavy guilt regarding that issue.

"Well," Hannah struggled to explain herself. "…if we do something good here, won't that make up for all the bad things?"

Hunter had listened to the conversation quietly, but Hannah's last statement cut to his heart. Tears came back to Hunter's eyes. Hannah was right.

Fifteen minutes later, the family was at the couple's back door again. Melvin opened the sliding glass door.

"We want to help," Hunter stated.

Melvin explained the hydroelectric facility was not far from where they were. A large tent had been set up in the chain linked facility. "When I visited there, they were keeping Robert, and six other workers who work for him, in that tent....well, I guess they all work for DHS now," Melvin stated in concession.

"Melvin, you know this place well?"

"Like the back of my hand."

"Is there a way to get into that place that no one would really think about?"

The rescue attempt was the topic of conversation at the Painter's kitchen table that morning with so many questions needing answered.

Where were the workers' families? Normal detention for "relocated" civilians was at the north of town. There were unconfirmed rumors that the original prisoners had been machine gunned in a quarry about two miles east of the confinement facility. Another rumor was that the families were considered to be useful leverage, so they were being kept at the Fredrick Medical Center. No one wanted to speak about the location of the families. To do so would invite harm on themselves and their loved ones. Only a few people might know the families' location. Perhaps the workers themselves did?

It was midnight. The two brothers had traveled almost three miles to the hydro plant. With them was Melvin, who kept up surprisingly well. Where Melvin and Hank stayed back from the facility a ways, Hunter found himself crawling in a drainage ditch toward the hydro facility with a pair of bolt cutters and a plastic bag. In the plastic bag was a note and a black fine point marker. The note read as follows:

> "This is Melvin Painter. We want to rescue you and your families, but we don't know where your families are. Our plan is to escape south as a group. We are awaiting your immediate reply."

Other than the bolt cutters and the note, Hunter was armed with only a .45 automatic and a knife, so he hoped he was not going to encounter any problems. He crawled on his belly the last two hundred feet along a ditch and arrived at his destination, a drainage culvert. Cutting the three wires that held the grate in place, Hunter pushed it aside and wormed his way through the two foot culvert. His more narrow frame allowed him to maneuver more readily than his brother. Although the running water was quite clean, the metal it ran across had nevertheless built up a sludge that was both slippery and odorous. Hunter slithered through the seventy-five feet from the perimeter opening. Not fifty feet, not a hundred feet. Melvin had been exact, but Hunter was not exactly sure how far he had traveled. Hunter's eyes had adjusted to the total darkness, which meant he could still see absolutely nothing. Every few feet of travel, he would lift his arm up, feeling for any opening in the top of the metal tunnel. His eyes strained, wide open, in search for some light. Was there something ahead, or his eyes playing tricks on his lack of vision? He reached up, and pushed forward. There. An opening. Hunter pushed forward again and looked upward. A dark overhead circle in a world of inky blackness. Hunter positioned himself awkwardly in the narrow space, stooped upward, and then silently lifted the drainage grate overhead.

Hunter returned to the tree-line ninety minutes later. In his hands, he had the worker's reply:

> "Our families are being held at the Southern Inn on Business 36. Some of us have visited them there. Same hotel each time. We are all in agreement with your plan and will do whatever you need."

That next day, a plan was being hashed out.

"We ensure the location of the families. We rescue the workers. We free the families. Then, take out the checkpoint leaving town. The only problem...we simply don't have the manpower." Hank was frustrated.

"Maybe we do," Hunter countered.

The hotel where the families were being kept captive was reconned, and detailed notes were taken. Two hummers, low profile security. It seemed that Homeland thought the town of Chillicothe was secure enough. The hotel was only about a mile from the hydro station. However, the hotel's exact position was near the intersection of two highways. This meant there was little vegetation or cover to protect the brothers from observation. Also, this part of town still had electricity and the hotel was well lit. It wasn't difficult determining which rooms held the captive families. Four rooms on that side had the lights on. Probably the windows were bolted closed and the doors locked on the outside. They would need those bolt cutters back from the workers.

The checkpoint on Highway 65 bridge was only half a mile from the hydro station. It was positioned on the town side of the bridge. Two hummers here, four men with what appeared to be M4s and a mounted M246 SAW. Sandbagged position. Concrete barriers were on the bridge to slow traffic. Hunter, however, had noted something about the fighting positions. "They are set up against vehicles on the road. Someone could come up the embankment or on that concrete ledge, behind the guardrail."

Correspondence was left for the hydro workers. The workers would be part of the rescue. They would all leave via the culvert immediately and attack before any nighttime headcount of the workers could be made and alerted to the escape. Even if the guards at the hydro station didn't notice the escape, they would be alerted as soon as the bridge checkpoint was attacked. The guards at the bridge checkpoint would have to be taken out quickly. The two hummers at the bridge were critical transportation. They would serve two purposes, the hummer with the mounted machine gun could stave off any enemy reinforcements from the hydro station. The other hummer would be wheeled to the Southern Inn to transport the families. The plan was to secure the humvee at the hotel.

"To be clear, all our transportation relies on our enemy resources. And we have limited firepower."

"Well, I don't know how much help it will be, but I do got my shotgun." Melvin stated, then he left through the back sliding door to go outside. The boys expected him to bring out a double barreled grandpa gun. They were pleasantly surprised when Mr. Painter returned with an 870 Remington Pump, along with a bag of shells. He opened the bag on the table: two boxes of slugs, two of buckshot. Then, he placed the shotgun on the table. "Extended 6 Tube," he mentioned quietly, touching the elongated tube magazine. "I wasn't quite ready to give this baby up."

"That will be quite helpful," Hank smiled his reply.

Chapter 5

Freedom

Two nights later, the plan went into action. This time Melvin, Martha, Hannah, and the two brothers all made the journey. Crossing under the highway through the "Coon Creek" culvert. Melvin, Martha, and Hannah remained hidden off the road at the entrance to the hydro station.

Hunter continued on to the hydro station, meeting the electric workers at the designated spot on the west side of the fence line. The workers had cut a single line in the chain link near the pole, then fastened the fence, making the cut hard to notice. Head count had been 15 minutes ago. They had 75 more minutes to pull off their mission. Hunter led the workers out of the electric plant, where they met up with Hank.

Hank took Melvin's son-in-law Robert, and two other workers. Armed with two pistols, and the shotgun, their job was to take the hotel by surprise. Hunter took the four other workers, all armed with assault rifles. If Hunter could not take the checkpoint, the brothers' plan would be a total bust.

Hunter's team made their way to the base of the bridge. Three armed workers stopped on that side of the bridge, while Hunter and one other rounded the bridge base to come in from the east. They were to crawl up the embankment unobserved, take position to eliminate enemy targets, and wait for Hunter.

Hunter's battle buddy snuck hunched against the base of the bridge, then crawled to a position where the concrete met the guardrail, about 40 feet from the guard shack, in order to support Hunter's movement. Hunter low-crawled to a position much closer to the guard shack. Once in position, Hunter noticed there seemed to be only one guard in the defensive position directly above him. The guard, who was smoking, was so close that Hunter could enjoy a remnant of the luxury lost to him.

"Change of plans," Hunter thought. He pulled out his hunting knife. Hunter leapt quietly over the steel guardrail and jumped at the guard.

God and Country

Frantically, Hunter struggled to cover the guard's mouth while drawing his knife. His intention was to slice the guard's throat, but his effort got the better of him, causing the knife in Hunter's right hand to miss its intended target. Instead, the knife embedded in the guard's neck. Blood squirted from the man's severed artery, and besides being unable to retrieve his hunting knife, the effect was the same. The guard slumped limp in front of him. Hunter slowly lowered the guard. As soon as the guard dropped, the other guard across the road yelled, and began firing at the position opposite him. Bullets hit the guardrail next to Hunter, pinging and sparking. Then, the worker near Hunter let out a three round burst with the M4 assault rifle. The three rounds landed short, hitting the sand bags. A triggered second burst, however, hit home at least twice.

Some say that the 5.56 round will tumble when it hits the body. That may be true. In this case, however, both rounds pushed through the guard's midsection. The first penetrated his chest, above the stomach, then exploded out the guard's back. Bits of spleen announced the exit of the deadly projectile. The second round hit right of the first, taking the guard center mass, shattering both his breastbone and two vertebrae. The third round went to the right further, a clean miss, probably the result of the marksman's overcompensation. The third round, however, was totally unnecessary, as the guard opposite Hunter was already dead.

Two assault rifles opened up on the other side of the road. It was the other team of workers. One single unarmed worker opposite Hunter leaped over the guardrail and into the opposite fighting position. He grabbed the dead DHS agent's assault rifle, lifted up, took good aim, and was instantly shot in the forehead, killing the worker. There were two more DHS agents in the vehicles parked up ahead. The two workers opposite Hunter were working their way down the guardrail toward the vehicles, using the railing for cover. A burst of automatic gunfire spattered 5.56 ball ammunition against the steel guardrail, pocking the metal rail with violent pings, but not penetrating.

Hunter lifted his rifle with a natural aim developed through years of hunting Iowa deer. Squeezing, Hunter dropped the DHS guard manning the turret mounted machine gun. The guard's body slumped over the weapon, pushing the muzzle high. Last reflexes of the dead gunner's hand triggered a sustained burst of 20 rounds firing over the heads of the two beleaguered workers. Missing their mark, the rounds fell into an ineffectual beaten zone on the river's floodplain far off.

The remaining guard was opening the door of the second hummer, parked across two lanes of the four lane road. He was poised over the Singuars radio set when Hunter walked up to the hummer. The guard looked pleadingly at Hunter, as he pointed the assault rifle at the man. For a fleeting second, Hunter was reminded of a scene from some movie he had watched a long time ago. Then a rage came over Hunter as he remembered what these men had done...what they had done to his wife. Hunter pulled the trigger. The guard's helmet was punched through by the high velocity round. Two more came immediately behind the last, creating a bloody mess not quite contained by the dead guard's helmet. "War is hell," Hunter thought, in an attempt to justify shooting the defenseless DHS agent.

Hunter could see the lights at the hydro station below. "Grab your rifles and follow me," Hunter shouted to the workers. He jumped into the first hummer, started it up, and floored the accelerator. His battle buddy was running next to him, banging on the passenger door. In the distance, Hunter could see vehicles from the hydro station carrying their rapid response team. He frantically waved his hands out the window, directing the second hummer to take up a defensive position at the hydro station entrance, in an attempt to thwart the enemy response force.

—

Hank and the three other men had been double-timing alongside the highway toward town, invisible to anyone on the raised highway next to them. They had a time schedule. They had jumped in the creek, ran under the highway, then began running toward Highway 36. As they approached the road, they had to lower their profile, hunching down, then crawling toward the concrete water culvert they had used to cross the highway before. Hank checked his watch. Fifteen minutes and Hunter would start his assault.

God and Country

Making their way to the parking lot, Hank noticed, like before, that all the guards seemed to be inside the hotel. Hank kept next to the hotel building itself, trying to blend in with the still existing, if somewhat a bit unkempt, landscape shrubbery. He noticed someone was there, next to a hummer. A uniformed DHS agent was talking to an attractive blonde, maybe in her thirties. She laughed at a joke, then looked up and saw Hank.

"Oh, shit!" Hank thought in a silent whisper.

But the woman said nothing. She laughed at the guard and turned toward him, angling herself closer, so the guard turned a bit to attend the woman better. Hank saw his opportunity and began to quietly come forward. The woman asked for a cigarette, then a light. The DHS agent was so preoccupied with the woman's cleavage that he was having difficulty lighting her smoke. Hank came up behind the guard, placed his 1911 .45 automatic up to the guard's temple, cocking back the single action hammer. The guard froze.

"Got another smoke?" Hank asked the guard. The guard, befuddled, nodded, and slowly pulled out another cigarette.

"Light?"

Hank's eyes met the guard and a silent understanding occurred. Hank would place an extra hole in the man's skull if he tried anything. The guard slowly lifted the lighter. Hank accepted the light, never losing eye contact.

"Now if you can follow directions, you will be the only one of your guys that makes it away from here alive. If you do not, you will die, and it will be an ugly death."

The three men of Hank's team made their way to Hank and his captive. Robert relieved the guard of his Glock 17. Hank pulled out the note that the workers had signed and showed it to the woman.

"Where is your husband's signature?"

The blonde pointed to the note.

"Where are the families?" The woman indicated to the three second floor lights that were on.

"And on the other side?"

45

God and Country

The woman nodded. Then she spoke: "I don't have a choice," the woman was trying to justify her actions. "They make us do this. If we don't do what they say, they punish us...or our husbands."

"I am not judging you. I am getting you out of here."

Hank brought the guard up to the door and had him knock. The door buzzed. When the DHS agent opened the door, Hank came in behind him with a pistol to the guard's head. Hank walked up to the agent. "I need the keys to the rooms. Now, and quietly." One worker walked behind the counter with the stainless .357 and pushed it into the guard's side. The agent nodded and put a small ring of keys on the counter, while discreetly pushing a doorbell, which buzzed. Unfortunately, the DHS agent was not discreet enough. The worker pulled the trigger of the large weapon, which in turn, produced large and lethal results. The expanding .357 hollow point at first met little resistance. Then, as the speeding round expanded, it pushed more and more bone and tissue ahead. By the time the round had passed through his intestines and exited the guard's body, an oversized mess of biomass splattered into the side cabinet. The guard collapsed in death like a sack of potatoes.

"Robert, watch him," Hank yelled, motioning to the other guard. "You both," Hank thumbed to the other two workers, "Back me up....and give me that." Hank traded his .45 for the Remington 870.

There was the pop of gunfire in the stairwell next to the office. Hank saw the exit sign at the far end of the first floor hall. He signaled for the two workers to go up the first stairwell, then sprinted past the stairwell down the hall, moving quietly up the back stairs. Reaching the second floor, Hank poked his head out and glanced down the hall. About 20 feet in front of him, a guard was intently watching his fellow agent fire his M4 down the front stairwell. Hank attempted to move quickly and quietly down the hall, but the closer agent heard this and turned to see Hank. Turning his assault rifle toward Hank, he managed to fire two rounds, which missed Hank's head by inches.

Simultaneously, Hank had fired a 12 gauge load of 00 buckshot at the guard's midsection. Hank's aim was also off. However, the 00 load of buckshot made a more forgiving pattern. The guard near Hank dropped his rifle, wounded. Down the hall, the other agent saw Hank, turned his weapon down the hall, and fired. Hank dropped. Two rounds hit the injured guard in front of Hank. The injured agent now dropped on the hallway floor dead. Hank began crawling on the floor toward the dead guard. The remaining guard seemed confused and fired another burst toward Hank. One round hit Hank's empty pistol holster, another impacted into the dead body providing him partial cover. Hank grabbed the dead agent's assault rifle from the floor, but by then the firefight was over. The confusion had allowed the two workers on Hank's team to round the corner of the stairwell. The agent had turned around to the stairwell again only to be greeted with .357 and .45 caliber rounds hitting his midsection. Pushed back by the impact, the agent slid down the hotel room door behind him.

The room doors had indeed been padlocked from the outside so Robert produced the bolt cutters to open each room. The occupants took place behind Hank's team until all doors had been opened. Fifteen women and children altogether filed behind the team downstairs, through the office, and outside.

Hank paused, secured the captive agent's arms behind his back with the office fax machine cord. As he knotted the cord tight, he told the prisoner. "You…" Hank pulled the knot again "…are to stay here until we leave. Understand?" Hank tied the agent's laces together. "No… moving…around!" Hank punctuated each word by cinching the agent's bonds.

The prisoner nodded.

Outside, the distant gunfire was clearly audible. Hank had noticed a second hummer parked to the side of the window.

"Robert, take another guy and find whatever food they have stored here. Guns, ammo. We have maybe 5 minutes, maybe less. Load whatever you find in the back of the hummers."

"You two, help me get these women and kids in the vehicles. Let's get ready to roll."

In three minutes, the women and children were inside the hummers.

God and Country

Robert and the other worker had not made their way back.

"Fuck!" Hank thought. He got out of the driver's seat of the first hummer and ran up to the office. The captive DHS agent had gotten up from the floor and was hopping down the hall.

"I don't have time for this," Hank thought to himself, walking up to the bound agent. "Just couldn't listen, could ya?" Hank exclaimed as he shot the escaping agent in the chest. "Robert, where the fuck are ya!" Hank yelled. "We gotta move!"

Hunter watched as the liberated humvee behind him swung into position. One worker, a red-headed fellow, had moved up to man the turret with the M240 machine gun. He traversed the weapon, trained it toward the oncoming relief force, and began laying down fire with an ease that suggested prior military experience. Hunter didn't know it yet, but former Army Specialist Ron Kaufman had spent four years with the 82nd Airborne Division. He was laying down an enfilade fire, plunging into his enemy target, just as he had been trained in Fort Bragg, and practiced in Iraq as a part of the 325th Airborne Infantry Regiment back in 2003. It seems that Kaufman's training was coming back to him.

Kaufman's well aimed fire caused the enemy relief vehicle to swerve hard, driving off the access road embankment about 125 yards away and hitting the opposite side of a drainage ditch hard. Another enemy vehicle following the first, pulled to the side of the narrow chat road. The second vehicle's occupants dismounted, but were immediately met with gunfire that forced them to take cover in the same ditch. At least for now, the enemy relief force had been effectively halted.

Hunter moved toward the town's southmost traffic light, which had been flashing red for the last two months. "Hey, buddy, got a name?" Hunter yelled to the worker riding shotgun.

The short, heavyset Hispanic fellow replied, "Pedro or Peter… whatever you want." There were tears in the worker's eyes. "Dat man that was shot back there. That was my brudder."

"Hey Pedro, I'm sorry. I really am."

God and Country

Hunter pulled into the hotel. Under the entrance awning was Hank and two men packing cardboard boxes in the back of hummers and then handing rifles to those inside.

Hunter spoke, opening the driver door by his brother. *"TWO hummers?"*

"See, we didn't need you here after all," Hank spoke in his own form of nonchalant, dry humor. "Nineteen people here altogether," Hank said to his brother. "How many with you?"

"Two here, five in position securing the hydro station," Hunter replied. "One of the workers..." Hunter shook his head.

Hank nodded understandingly. "We got to roll."

The back of Hunter's vehicle was hastily filled with a few remaining boxes of MRE's; then the convoy rolled out of the hotel parking lot with Hank's vehicle in the lead.

As the lead hummer turned at the intersection, Robert, who rode shotgun, remarked to Hank, "You got headlights to the south. Looks like a response force. Can't be good." The convoy picked up speed, then slowed again as it approached the hydro station entrance.

Again the convoy stopped when Hank saw a man jump down from a hummer's machine gun turret. Robert opened the passenger door, and Kaufman spoke to Hank, his voice booming. "I sent Melvin, Martha, and the girl up to the checkpoint to secure weapons. Seemed the right thing to do." A bullet hit the turret of the hummer behind him. Then another.

Kaufman looked behind, then continued. "Looks like you got company coming for ya. You go ahead and move across that bridge. We will fall in behind ya. I got a little something for those DHS bastards when they try to come for us." The lights of pursuing vehicles were about a half mile away. Kaufman banged his fist twice on Hank's vehicle, swiftly swung up his own hummer's hood, and was in the gunner's turret again, amid freshly erupting gunfire from the access road. When the convoy had passed, Kaufman's vehicle turned and followed them. Then, Kaufman's vehicle began to fall back. He was firing the M240 directly into the path of

God and Country

the oncoming pursuers. The DHS vehicles slowed, backing off a bit, but never quite stopped chasing.

Hank was at the checkpoint. Two workers stepped out and helped load rifles, MOLLE gear, and boxes in the back of the hummers.

"Go, go, go!" Hunter exclaimed as he grabbed Hannah and looked back at Kaufman's approaching vehicle. Three workers finished loading, or better said, overloading the hummers with material. The hummers made their way around the concrete Jersey barricades, which were totally blocking two lanes of the four lane bridge. More Jersey barriers and traffic barrels narrowed down the two remaining lanes, requiring a slow twisting. The three vehicles moved through the winding exit just as Kaufman's machine gun went dead.

The enemy vehicles again started their pursuit. Kaufman's vehicle went around the elaborate barriers and began taking gunfire from the DHS agents following them. Then, Kaufman's vehicle stopped in the middle of the bridge. The first of the pursuing vehicles, a M1078 troop carrier, began to round the barricades. Atop the troop carrier, a machine gunner was traversing his turret mounted weapon, the legendary Maw Deuce. The mounted .50 caliber M2 machine gun could put an end to the entire convoy. But Kaufman also had a hand to be played. A lone figure stepped out of Kaufman's hummer. In his hand was what appeared to be an elongated tube. The figure held the front of the tube by some sort of a pistol grip. His right hand steadied the tube. He peered down a small aperture and fired the device. An 82 millimeter high-explosive projectile exploded from the front of the tube just as the DHS machine gunner began to open fire. Fifty caliber rounds impacted just a few feet from Kaufman's hummer when the high-explosive projectile reached its target. An orange fireball appeared, engulfing the vehicle's driver, the machine gun operator, and twenty DHS agents in the back of the vehicle.

The heat blast, followed closely by a subsequent explosion of deafening violence, awoke the darkness. Kaufman nodded, smiled, and reentered the hummer, which then sped away to catch the renegade convoy. Driving through the forest darkness, it was almost six miles before

God and Country

Kaufman saw the red lens flashlight waving up ahead. He followed the red flashlight, turning onto a gravel county road to the left.

"I am glad this was you," Hunter said to Kaufman. "Otherwise I would be one dead, dumb ass."

The vehicles had parked along the gravel road. The people had gathered on the desolate road. Hunter stood atop Hank's front hummer and waved his flashlight. "Hey, guys. We need everyone to the front."

The people moved forward and became quiet, except for someone crying in the back of the group. Then total silence. It began to mist, and droplets began to form on Hank's head. He began to speak.

"I am Hank, this is my brother Hunter, and his daughter Hannah." Spontaneous applause broke about among the small group. Hank waited, then spoke again. "Look, guys, your husbands might have told you already that they wanted us to help get you out. We don't normally do shit like this. We did it because…" Hank looked down at Hannah. "….because we know what it's like. We have lost family…recently. I know some of you have tonight. I am sorry, and there ain't no words, I know." Hank stopped and put his head down.

Hunter continued for him. "We're from Iowa, headed to Arkansas. We didn't plan on any of this. You can stay with us a while if you want." The brothers spoke ineloquently, yet with a certain modest and simple sincerity that the group recognized.

It would get morning soon, and the convoy was only 8 miles from Chillicothe, from where they had escaped. "Not exactly a great place to be at," Hunter shared with his brother a few minutes later. "If they find us, they will kill all of us."

Chapter 6

Need

"We need an inventory. Who was that guy that did all of that Navy Seal shit back there?"

"Kaufman," there was a voice behind them. Kaufman walked up to their vehicle and placed his forearms on the wet hood of the vehicle, mimicking the two brothers.

"How did you know how to use that gun and...was that an explosion we saw?"

Kaufman told the brothers of his military experience. He had worked at the power station for 10 years after returning from Iraq, and his family had been one of the lucky few who had not been sent to the correctional facility north of town.

"We hear DHS agents talk at the station. They never worried about us listening. Arrogant pricks. Homeland came through here and wanted to clear Highway 65 down to Springfield. For some reason they couldn't get past the Missouri River. They were stopped at Miami. That was about a month ago. Our town was having enough problems already. No food. People eating their dogs; it was so bad. The town council was putting together an emergency resolution to pool resources, when DHS came back north and stopped here. They moved the people out of their homes. I guess they didn't want some sort of rebellion."

"Kaufman, you know weapons, right?"

The red-headed man nodded.

"Can you get with Martin and help us determine our weapons situation? We are gonna have to stay around here today and might need to defend ourselves."

"Well, if I were you, I would move the vehicles to right below the ridge, inside that small forest area." Kaufman indicated to the southeast side of the road. "Give you a good view of anyone approaching. We could set up lookouts."

"Do you know anything about the radios that are in the hummers?" Hunter asked.

Kaufman gave a dry smile and nodded.

After getting a bit of troubled sleep, the brothers met with Melvin, Robert, and three other workers, Pedro, Evans, and Mr. Stephens. Kaufman and Martin were still pulling watch.

The power plant workers had mixed feelings about what to do.

"We have family members in Chillicothe. My mother...," Evans expressed his concern.

"They treated us well because of our jobs. The others are treated like animals," Pedro added.

"We want you to stay with us. Help us fight these bastards that are hurting our town."

"Hank and Hunter have already done more than we could have ever thought possible," the elderly, Mr. Painter spoke up. "We need to let them go where they need to go."

It was agreed to meet later that evening to discuss different concerns of the group.

About a half a mile from where they had turned off the highway, Hank and Hunter walked down a fence line to where Kaufman and Martin had established an observation post. The hummer was parked in a rocky wash on the hidden side of the ridge under the same group of cedar trees where Kaufman lay sleeping. Martin was alert to their presence.

"What in the hell is that thing?" Hank pointed to a tube contraption angled toward the visible highway.

The words awoke Kaufman. "That is a mortar system. Specifically the M224."

"It shoots... mortars?" Hunter enquired, realizing immediately he sounded stupid.

"Yup. Better said, it launches 60 millimeter high explosive cartridges." He patted an extra large ammo can. "It was in the back of the hummer. I might not be the best person to operate this equipment, but if I

God and Country

get a good aiming point, I can drop close to 20 mortars in a minute at that intersection and create a hell of a mess firing in defilade."

"I don't know what most of that means," Hunter confessed.

Kaufman simply smiled and nodded his head. He was obviously in his element. Kaufman gave them a written list of their arms and ammunition. The list read:

    8 M4s assault rifles
    4 M16s assault rifles
    1 M240 machine gun
    1 M203 grenade launcher mounted
    2 beretta 9mm pistol
    9mm SIG Sauer P226 with silencer
    96 rounds of 9mm
    About 7 full combat loads (210/7 mags)
    5.56 with 2,520 extra rounds (bandoliers with clips)
    36 rounds (combat load) HE 40mm grenades
    2 crates M19 linked belt 7.62 (16 belts/1600 rds)
    1 .357 revolver (94 rounds)
    1 .45 (50 rounds)
    8 hand grenades M67

Over the next two days, Kaufman spent most of his time at the observation post. He gave basic rifle marksmanship to people who would rotate in, both men and women. He provided basic training on the operation of the M240 machine gun. People that couldn't fire a rifle before understood the basics of loading, firing, and how to perform immediate action on the weapons. They understood a good sight picture and could properly aim and fire their weapon. Or so it seemed. Not one actual shot had been fired.

There was no sign of Homeland those two days. The mist changed to a light drizzle, then back to mist. It was as if the weather itself was holding off, waiting for something. The boxes of MRE's had been rationed, with each person receiving only one ration per day. Children received half rations. Hank, Hunter, and Hannah did not touch the rations, only eating the food in their packs. People rested, sleeping the best they could in the vehicles during the daytime. The children were restless.

Pedro had volunteered to recon the area for food and shelter. He came back having spotted what appeared to be an abandoned farmhouse about two miles distant. No sign of the occupants. Hank and Hunter went back with Pedro to investigate further. As they traveled, the trio walked and talked.

"We can't simply leave, though." The conversation went.

"Some want to stay here. Others want to go." Pedro said with his thick Mexican accent. "My wife, children, and my sister-in-law….we want to go. Missouri is not home for us. I cannot imagine what Matamoros would be like now. Our family wants to go to Arkansas."

Hank eyed the steel gray clouds to the west covering the sun of late afternoon sky, "Well, from the looks of that, we ain't going nowhere anytime soon."

The farmhouse was indeed in the middle of nowhere, just as Pedro had described. It was an older, two-story wooden clapboard home with narrow rooms and two side porches, one for each level. The roof looked good, and although the outside brown walls looked in need of a good repainting, it definitely seemed habitable. Hank checked the door. A new lock and doorknob seemed mismatched for the antique wooden door. Hank was muttering something about checking back and breaking a window when Hunter noticed the door mat's message: "Hello, I'm Mat!" the porch rug read.

Hunter smiled and lifted up the corner of the mat, finding a key. Inside, the house seemed to have been vacated. The front room had been decorated by a person who must've had an obsession with both sunflowers and The Three Stooges. Odd combination. The kitchen was fully stocked with everything except food. The three bedrooms were small, but there were several blankets in the house. This could work for now.

God and Country

The gray sky was almost dark with not a hint of sunset. The drizzle that had hung on and off in the air was colder now. They needed to get here tonight. Two hours later, after dusk, the four hummers loaded up and within ten minutes made the two miles to the farmhouse. The people dismounted their vehicles and began settling into the house. An observation post/defensive position was set up at the base of the drive, with it, the sole avenue of approach to the house, being watched by the M240 machine gun.

"You do realize that we have 27 people here, right?" Hank asked Hunter as the two sat outside on the porch, looking at the long drive which led to the invisible road some half mile distant.

"What is your point?" Hunter, like everyone else, was tired and emotionally drained.

"We gotta be able to feed 'em. The people are going through three boxes of MREs per day. What happens in nine more days? Hell, we only have enough dry food for maybe two more weeks ourselves."

"Well, what the hell do you propose we do about it? Go back into town and get shot at again?" questioned Hunter.

"Everyone knows where all the food is being kept. The same place where all the supplies are kept. Winmart," Melvin said.

Which made sense. Winmarts were near dead center to any town's transportation hub, in this case on the south side of town, near the hotel where the families had been rescued. The discount chain had located their store near both Highway 36 and 56, making transporting goods more efficient. In a time of peace or emergency, efficiency mattered. That was only logical. On the other hand, the correctional facility, the high school, the medical facility, and the National Guard unit were on the north side of town. The response force chasing the escape convoy had come from the north side, as well.

As the conversation continued, plans began to be made for the second raid of Chillicothe. In later years, the people of the town would refer to it as "The Great Winmart Run."

Plans were drawn. Scouts were sent. Materials were gathered.

God and Country

Over the next week, Melvin and Martha watched the children while Kaufman undertook the job of training his 15 students. Fundamentals of marksmanship, basic fire and maneuver, immediate action and remedial action of weapon systems were all drilled into the team. Angie, who was a registered nurse, gave classes on how to give CPR, stop bleeding, and protect the wound. After a somewhat lengthy discussion, Kaufman effectively argued that everyone drive 15 miles south and conduct a live fire training event.

"You can't expect a person to fire an M4 for the first time in combat," Kaufman maintained.

During this week, Hank began to notice that his brother, Hunter, had stopped eating and never seemed to get any rest. At the impromptu firing range, Hank confronted his brother.

"You are looking pretty thin and worn out, man."

"It's a new weight loss plan," Hunter responded, slipping sarcasm into his words. "Just have some crazy bastard blow up your wife, then go on a massive killing spree, and plan yet another. It'll take the weight off ya every time."

"Just don't go trying to do something crazy."

"We are planning on murdering at least ten people to go grocery shopping! How crazy is that?" Hunter smiled as he spoke the words.

"You know we need that food," Hank interjected.

"Yeah. And a part of me wants all the fucking bastards to die a slow death, but when does it all end?"

"Dunno. Maybe when all the bad guys die?" Hank offered uneasily.

—

The plan was as follows:

A five-man infiltration team led by Kaufman, would silently enter Winmart by the back way. Their master tool, a cordless drill and titanium bits. Just in case, however, a 16 lb hammer, crowbar, and flat head ax were backup tools. Many suggestions were given as to how to cross the river with such heavy tools. However, upon a scout of the nearby abandoned town of Utica, a three dollar blowup air mattress promised to fit the bill

God and Country

fine. The team would use 35-gallon trash bags to float themselves across the river. They would enter the building, take out any interior guards and assist any attack by other teams at the front entrance of Winmart. If possible, they would ready goods for transport out the side service entry. Two members of the infiltration team would engage the exterior guards when the 36 Bridge was engaged. Overwhelming force would be brought when the 36 Bridge team arrived.

The attack team consisted of 3 members armed with assault rifles and hand grenades. They would ford the river at the same river bend at the same time as the infiltration team. Maneuvering to the Highway 36 bridge, they would await a signal, eliminate the guard post at Highway 36 bridge, and clear the way for transportation. Any vehicles or weapons that could be hastily retrieved would be done.

The transportation/backup team would be a 4 man team with two hummers and an eighteen-wheeled semi trailer truck found at Utica. The first hummer would engage the Highway 36 checkpoint from across the bridge being backed up by the attack team, who would use hand grenades to eliminate the checkpoint.

A three-person team would be a diversion. They would await the radio signal of the infiltration team. Its job would be to attack the National Guard unit on the north of town. They would "stir the hornet's nest" so to speak. The team would drive a truck, a white Chevy Silverado Crewcab 4x4, west and lead off as many pursuit vehicles as they could, attempting to lose their pursuers in dirt/mud paths along the river.

Most every man and woman would be needed for this. Mr. and Mrs. Painter would watch over the ten children. Not knowing who would return, if anyone, the older couple promised to take care of each and every child as their own. Farewells were made. It was time.

After the attack teams were briefed by Kaufman, Hunter spoke up and addressed the group around a small fire. "We know you are not soldiers…and we are not fighting for a country or flag. But, we are husbands, wives, fathers and mothers. We are fighting for our families, for the ability to survive this winter. I can't think there is a greater cause than

God and Country

that." Then, almost as an afterthought, Hunter added "May God be with us."

The group lingered, and Hank, Hunter, and Kaufman walked away from the crowd a bit. Kaufman turned to Hunter and said: "Hell, a couple weeks ago, you planned and successfully conducted a complex military operation with only one casualty. I ain't a church-goin' man, but I would say God is already with you."

Hank took in Kaufman's comment. Sure, they had been lucky. But, they had suffered loss. Hunter had lost his wife; Hannah, her mother. And that woman, what was her name, Catalina? She had lost her husband. As if on cue, Hank looked up and saw her watching the three of them. By the firelight, Hank saw her force a small, sad smile. Her eyes still filled with hurt and loss. A hurt that Hank knew all too well. Hank swore that he would never hurt like that again.

On November 21st, three men of the infiltration team entered the Lube and Tire Express rear entrance of the Winmart at 1065 Raves Street in Chillicothe, Missouri. Kaufman jimmied the slide lock of a service window and climbed inside the main building. There was a low level of lighting throughout the store. The three-man team waited. Pedro motioned that he heard footsteps. Pedro intentionally dropped an air pressure gauge onto the floor. The footsteps came closer. The guard walked into the Auto Service area, then dropped dead, his brain being scrambled by Kaufman using an old Mark 2 combat knife. Kaufman smiled as he let the guard drop to the floor. Silently, they waited. There must be a security room here. Taking it out quietly would be key. He looked around. There it was, at the front of the store, above "Customer Service" were 6 mirrored windows.

Behind the Automobile Service Center counter, the team busily undressed a DHS uniformed guard, who happened to be dripping blood profusely from the base of his skull. Five minutes later, a new uniformed guard, Kaufman, was walking past a previously ransacked, but now quiet pet care section, bare shelves of a pharmacy, and toward the front of the

59

God and Country

store. Kaufman smiled as he passed a banner which proclaimed "Always the Lowest Prices." He was enjoying this.

  Fifteen minutes later, two more interior guards had been eliminated and the store was clear. Then came the search. Located behind the empty meat section of the grocery, the infiltration team found double-stacked pallets of MREs. Cream of wheat, corn, sugar, pasta. Canned meats. In another section clearly marked "Detainment Facility," they found pallets of what looked to be 50 pound sacks. Upon closer inspection, Kaufman could make out the label. "Ol Max" the top sack declared its contents, along with the picture of a laughing golden retriever. "Sonofabitch," Kaufman said out loud. Kaufman left Pedro in the side warehouse area with instructions. He and Martin walked quickly to the front of the store, drawing their pistols. Holding open a small glass door, Kaufman followed Martin. They both took positions, waiting, finding two guards in a hummer parked next to a broken and overturned Pepsi machine. He placed the SIG Sauer in the waistband of his pants at the small of his back and carried his handheld AN/PRC 148 in his left hand, walking toward the hummer. Waving his radio at the two guards, the driver opened the door. Kaufman pushed the radio at the man as if to hand it to him. Simultaneously reaching to the small of his back, Kaufman drew the silenced P226 from his back and shot two times. Unlike in the movies, a pistol silencer does not make a 9mm handgun sound silent. It simply reduces the noise somewhat. The two loud pops sounded with devastating results. With one guard missing a good portion of his brain in the passenger seat, and the driver choking and losing blood quickly through a horrific neck wound, their attacker, Army Specialist Ron Kaufman lifted his radio: "It's time."

  Two other members of the infiltration team engaged what appeared to be a guard position at the front entrance of the Winmart parking lot. The guards had walked out to investigate some popping noises. The two guards dropped immediately from five well-aimed shots of recently-trained marksmen. Both guards were wounded, one severely. One guard had his hands up; the other was on the ground, groaning loudly. The two outside members of the infiltration team ran up, training their weapons on the two fallen guards.

Another shot rang out. One of the team members was hit, and fell. The two attacking workers took cover behind the guard shack, one helping his other injured colleague. It looked to be a shoulder wound. An oddly timed, almost rhythmic, shootout began. There would be a single shot from the one remaining DHS agent taking cover in the Winmart lawn section, then a burst of three or four rounds from the aggressing team members. Almost a perfectly explosive pattern by which one could two-step, or perhaps waltz. All of this rhythm was accompanied by the loud groaning of the mortally wounded agent lying on the asphalt. A cross fire of sorts developed from the differently positioned attackers. It was apparent that the single armed DHS guard was low on ammunition as his shots grew fewer. Hearing the explosions at the bridge in the background, the lone guard realized that his situation was hopeless. He lifted his hands up, threw an empty 9mm pistol on the pavement, and waited.

Kaufman walked up to him and shot him in the head at point blank range. Pedro was horrified. Kaufman kept walking toward the guard shack, again he raised his pistol. His two team members behind the guard shack were aghast. They had never seen their colleague, their friend, like this. Kaufman would have killed the last guard standing had it not been for Pedro. Pedro shouted something in Spanish, Kaufman turned, and there Pedro was holding his own pistol not three feet from Kaufman's head. Kaufman lowered his pistol, rubbed his face and eyes as if to clear away a fog, and sat down on the pavement, weeping. The one standing guard was shaking, having pissed his pants. The other DHS guard then groaned his last note and exhaled one final time.

The taking of Bridge 36 checkpoint had been somewhat easy. Although the guards had been alert, they were instantly engaged by the 7.62 rounds suddenly assaulting them from across the river. They were distracted by the gunfire at the Winmart a half mile away. Then the attack team threw three grenades, having been cooked off for an airburst effect. The results were deadly. Having seen the explosions, the machine gun across the bridge stopped, and the hummer came forward. Two of the guards lay on the ground, dead. Another was nearing the same end, as two spots of blood on his uniform top grew larger. He was crying, saying something about his mother. In one of the hummers, a single DHS agent was watching outside the front passenger window. Facing him were the three members of the attack team and a turret-mounted M240 pointed directly at him. He lifted his hands and opened the door.

The attack team had stripped the weapons off the dead soldiers and piled them to the side. One attack team member, Angie, was to secure the checkpoint and gather up other supplies left behind. The other members of the attack team started up the newly liberated hummers and began their midnight Winmart run with the transportation team following behind.

Within four minutes after the signal had been given, the semi tractor trailer had driven around the retail building and parked along its side, ready to be loaded. Martin had already rolled open the 12-foot blue warehouse door and had a double stack pallet of MREs on his forks. He began loading the pallets with the ease of someone who had loaded freight for years. In fact, he had. Martin had spent many autumn nights driving a forklift, stacking bales at several cotton compresses in east Mississippi.

Meanwhile, north of town, Robert had chosen to split from his other two team members. His men knew the route along the river. They could make it. He would use the grenade launcher to assault the front of the Guard Center, creating a distraction. His two team members lay in wait outside the fence on the south side of the armory. At the signal, Robert shotgunned a 40 millimeter grenade into the launcher, charging the trigger. Then he fired. The heavy popping sound surprised Robert, who had expected an explosion. The first grenade was high on the main building, and exploded on impact on a trailer containing a ten kilowatt generator set. The explosion, nevertheless, did the job to get the attention of the inside occupants. Robert pushed the silver detent latch that popped open the carriage of the launcher, placed another in, and launched it with success into the left center window, breaking the window and putting a high explosive fireball over the "ARM" of the Armory sign.

God and Country

    People began to run out the back of the center toward the small motor pool. Not guardsmen, though. The last of the Missouri National Guardsmen at Chillicothe had either been executed, imprisoned, or were missing. These were DHS agents, wearing their black tactical uniforms. "They had no business here," Robert thought. The two other members of his distraction team, Lola and Delores, lay grazing fire in the agents' direction. Where perhaps only a couple of bullets hit their mark in the darkness, nevertheless, several agents went down from the effect of deadly defilade fire.

    Another explosion, Robert began to run in their direction. To their north, on Highway 65, Robert could see a group of vehicles beginning to make their way from the correctional facility. He joined his team, working the grenade launcher with better practice now. Robert looked at Lola. She had just loaded another fresh thirty round magazine home and was unloading its contents, in three-round bursts, toward the emerging agents. Robert, unable to see the leaf sight of his launcher, reckoned his target and fired away. A HEMTT refueling tanker took a direct rear hit, and began to burn. The diesel would not explode. It did, however, light the target better and add to the agent's confusion. Robert then yelled: "Lola, you both go now! I've got this!"

    Lola tried to say something in reply, but Robert had already left, running across the side of a warehouse, intentionally silhouetting himself. Bullets flew around him, he dove and crawled for the corner of the building. Here he could see the worker convoy of trucks moving out, about a mile south in the distance. Lola and Delores had made their way to the Silverado and paused at the other side of the warehouse. Robert waved them off, shouting above the gunfire: "Go!" The two members of the distraction team did not leave, but began taking up fighting positions behind the white pickup. There was a vehicle attempting to leave the motor pool onto the highway. Robert, with grenade sight visible now, lobbed a round at the cab of the hummer. It exploded. The vehicles were lined up now with no place to go. Robert loaded another grenade, aimed, and shot a five ton troop carrier. The round exploded directly on top of the men in the cargo area. "Like shooting fish in a barrel." Robert went forward to assault another motor pool vehicle, then moved more to the highway. He again waved his two team members away.

"Go....Please!"

Lola looked over to Delores, who was firing her assault rifle at a hummer pulling out of the parking lot. Part of her wanted to take as many of these "maldito bastardo" with her, yet another part knew she could not let Delores down. They had to go. The two looked one last time at Robert as the DHS vehicles bore down on him, then turned right slowly, waiting for the enemy convoy to see the taillights of their truck.

Now according to an old Scottish poem, "The best-laid plans of mice and men often go awry." Or, perhaps better quoted, would be a line from the 70s rock ballad: "Nothing ever goes as planned." Indeed one thing the brothers' plan had failed to count on was the response from the hydro plant. No longer with its workers to keep the electricity flowing, the plant was still functioning, limping along so to speak. DHS agents had brought more workers to stay there, men who tried to upkeep the maintenance of the facility to little effect. However, the ten-man response force had been beefed up there, and now was twenty man strong.

Hunter sped his hummer to the intersection and turned south to engage the hydro plant's response force, a four-hummer team that was making its way up onto Highway 65. He began firing the M240 at the emerging vehicles.

Inside Winmart, Martin was loading the last of 8 pallets, a small one labeled "Saint Peter's Des Moines Medical Center." Martin backed the forklift off the semi, rolled the door shut, and banged the side of the trailer, yelling something loud in Spanish. More automatic gunfire sounded now, closer than before. Martin jumped onto the bumper of the semi, holding onto the side of the trailer as the semi took off. Rounding the corner a bit too close, the semi-trailer succeeded in clearing the building only after a scraping bump that managed to knock Martin off the back of the trailer.

God and Country

Falling and cursing, Martin got back up, and running with a limp, barely managing to regain his position on the back of the vehicle.

At the front of the parking lot, Hank and the remaining others were watching what looked like a major gun battle unfold on Highway 65. As the semi tractor trailer rolled to the front of the store, he directed one hummer to follow the semi across the bridge. Hank sped away east, rounding the intersection, and raced toward the storm of gunfire.

—

Hunter had taken a firing position on the front passenger side of his vehicle, using his door as cover. Suddenly, he noticed that his vehicle's machine gun had stopped firing.

"It's jammed!" the gunner cried.

"Fix it!" came Hunter's reply.

"I can...."

The gunner's sentence was cut short as a 7.62 round caught the worker in the throat, exploding his neck vertebrae. He hung there lifeless. Hunter knew he had to get the machine gun operational. He entered the vehicle, pulled the bloody corpse from the weapons station, and attempted immediate action. "POPP," Hunter whispered to himself quietly, as rounds whizzed past him. "Pull, Observe, Push, and Press," was the immediate action Kaufman had taught them. Nothing.

Hunter turned around to look at the distant Winmart store and noticed the semi trailer had pulled onto Highway 36. The woman who had taken Hunter's previous fighting position was dead, the door's ballistic glass having been spider-webbed and finely penetrated by several 7.62 rounds. The driver looked up at Hunter from her position and shook her head. The enemy hummers were now rolling again, two abreast, throwing a deadly hail of lead.

Then suddenly, from behind, yet more gunfire. Hunter turned his head to see a hummer approaching in the next lane. Atop in the weapons station, Hunter saw his brother. Hank was screaming something, firing the 7.62 machine gun. The image was to burn into Hunter's mind and later reminded him of some war-crazed Viking warrior of the past. Then, Hunter felt his left arm explode in a fiery pain, and he blacked out.

Chapter 7

Shelter

"Hunter has a large piece of his tricep missing, but I am keeping it cleanly dressed and the ampicillin seems to be working. There may be a slight fracture to his humerus, however, there is little I can do for that right now. Bleeding was kept to a minimum by that improvised tourniquet. Becky did well."

"Angie, it was you who trained her," Hank replied, already knowing the next question Angie would ask.

"Any word from Robert?" Despair was barely hidden in Angie's voice.

Hank shook his head sadly.

Angie stiffened her chin to hold back trembling, but a single tear appeared in her eye, threatening to drop. Finally, it did.

Hank's mind wandered. There had been losses in the last raid. Two people killed, his brother injured, and Robert...well they just didn't know what happened to him. This was not a game; Hank understood that people died. But recently, Hank seemed somehow numb, perhaps some self-defense mechanism against the pain. Angie's tears, Mr. Evans' and Mrs. Stephens' losses, the three children who would never see their mom or dad again, they all were simply stifled hammer blows echoing against the numbness of his soul. Only Jorge's widow, Catalina, had seemed to awaken his heart to the pain. That, and his injured brother.

Hannah walked in. She had a basket full of straw and colorful leaves, carefully arranged with acorns and pine cones. Centered in the middle of the basket was a small crucifix. "Is my dad awake yet?"

"Not yet, sweetie. What ya got there?"

"I made it for Daddy. For Thanksgiving."

Hank scratched his head. Honestly, although it had been only a month since they had left Clarinda, he had lost all track of days. They were all the same. Thanksgiving? Really? Hank found himself lost in a mist of memories. Memories of his last Thanksgiving with Abigail. Had it really been four years? Everyone was at Grandma Tammy's, even ol Gramps and Granny. Granny had been trying to teach Abi how to make gravy. And, little Hannah was getting all the attention. Mom, Jason, and Haley had made the trip from Arkansas. Abi loved the holidays when everyone was together. She especially loved Thanksgiving.

Hank and Abi had been high school sweethearts and were planning on starting a family, when Abi got sick. When Abi died, Hank had been devastated. Even now, the feeling of loss ached like an old battle scar. Healed and the pain gone, but memories of the hurt were still there.

Hunter stirred in his bed. His head turned toward the sound of Hannah's voice and his eyes opened.

"Hi Daddy." Hannah lifted up the basket. "Happy Thanksgiving," the girl said uncertainly.

"It's beautiful," Hunter replied weakly. Hannah's eyes beamed the special love that only a daughter has for her father.

"Ms. Martha had us all decorate these for Thanksgiving. She said we had a lot to be thankful for. And I am. I like it here. It's just...I miss Mom."

"I know, Baby Girl. Me, too." Hunter's eyes grew misty, then they closed. Suddenly an overwhelming wave of fire and ache hit him, both physically and emotionally.

This was what Hunter was to feel for the next several weeks. For the first time in over two weeks, Hunter had been on the go, always doing something to take his mind off of his recent loss. Why had he trusted SSG Panning? It would make the pain more bearable if he could blame anyone else, yet he had done this. His wife, had she really loved him? He had indeed loved her and wanted to make it work. Now he never could. His wife was dead.

Then there was the physical pain. The strongest pain medication to be had was ibuprofen. Hunter had a gunshot wound that had removed an inch of flesh from his left arm. At first it was a burning fire and ache. Later on, as Hunter would begin to heal, there would be less fire and more

God and Country

of an achy, itching sensation. At first, Hunter was overwhelmed by the pain, but, over time, he learned to accept it, even embrace it as a penance of sorts to somehow pay for his horrible mistake.

And throughout all those times, Hannah would visit, come hold his hand. She would make him laugh for a moment. When afterwards, Hunter would start weeping uncontrollably, Hannah would cry with him. She would console her father as if he were a younger brother sometimes. After all, she, of all people, understood.

Yet there was another person who was missing a loved one in the room, Angie. Some people say that not knowing what happened to a spouse is more difficult than knowing that they died. Angie's thoughts about Robert obsessed her. She worked nursing Hunter, changing his bandages and cleaning his wound, but the thought of what had happened to her husband never seemed to leave.

Angie spoke to Hank outside in the hall. "Hunter will not lose his arm," Angie informed Hank. "In fact, it seems Hunter will have full function of his arm. His tendons appear undamaged."

Hank nodded.

"And about Robert," Angie continued. "We are going to get him back?"

Hank nodded in reply, not saying a word. Hank knew the likely truth. Robert was either dead, or worse. The fact that this little ragtag rebel group had not been located thus far indicated Robert was most likely dead. Almost three weeks had passed since the Winmart run.

"Hank?" Angie was standing directly in front of him.

Hank's eyes met hers. "We will find him," Hank said unconvincingly, turned, and walked out of the room.

—

Hunter awoke to find frost on the bedroom window. His wound was healing more now. The itch of knitting flesh now accompanied the ache of trauma, driving him crazy at times. Hannah had come into the room bundled up in her blanket, blowing the cold smoke of the coming winter, pretending to be a steam locomotive. She was looking like the little girl he had always known. Hunter realized, however, that his little girl had been carrying a burden most adults would buckle under. She seldom mentioned her mother to him, but he knew Hannah felt the loss as he did. Yet, that injury, like his arm, would knit and mend with time.

Angie had been quieter than usual. Hank had gone out three times looking for word of Robert's location. In the last two weeks, Hank had surveilled both the prison and the post office, but there appeared to be no sign of him. As a result, Angie was weighted down, going through the drudgeries of a life with no meaning.

Angie returned to the bedroom where Hunter had been staying. She knelt, resting her hand on Hunter's bed. "Your arm is mending well. I won't need to check on you after today. Simply keep your dressing clean," Angie told Hunter

"Thank you," Hunter replied sincerely. Somehow it seemed right to move his hand and place it on hers. Angie looked at Hunter and gave a slight smile. "You're welcome." She lingered there a moment, then, as if startled, got up and left.

Hunter could not help but notice how much Angie reminded him of his late wife. Not her hair, nor the way Angie acted. Actually, it was her eyes. Yet, Angie's eyes were loving, healing. They were…beautiful.

That night, the two brothers talked.

"Have you noticed the weather?" Hank asked with a tight grin on his face. "That wall cloud right there." Hank pointed a well-muscled arm toward the northwest over the ridge of the hill. "That is going to mean some snow."

Hunter had been up and around enough just to appreciate how busy Hank had been. Blankets were in short supply; they were one of the necessities that one does not think about when conducting a paramilitary raid. Not that there had been any extra time to strip the sheets at the local hotel, or stroll through the local discount store in the bedding section. Clothing, however, was somewhat easier to find, and had already been used to form makeshift mattresses on the bedroom floors. He had the workers

God and Country

bring bales of hay from the barn and stacked it on the north and west sides of the house. Plastic in whatever form, shrink-wrap salvaged from the pallets, tarpaulins, feed bags, had all been used to cover the windows. Wood that had already been cut and seasoned in the shed had been brought up to the porch for the small stove. Hank had been preparing for an extended battle against the upcoming cold of winter. Indeed, even the squirrels and birds seemed to be unusually busy in preparation against the yet unseen weather.

"Hank," Hunter stated, oblivious to what his brother was saying. "We have to leave."

"Leave. Why?"

"We have to find mom, Jason, and Haley. I am better now."

"Are we living in the same reality? There is bad weather coming. We have a place to hole up here. We actually have food. Besides, what about the families?" Hank referred to the some twenty men, women, and children they had rescued. "What about Melvin and Martha?"

Hunter thought and slowly nodded. Of course Hank was right. Why was he wanting to leave, to…run away?

—

"I don't want it! God take it away! Ahhh! Go away!"

It was the first snow of the winter that early December morning. Most everyone had been in the living room, huddled around the small wood stove. They were distracted by the screaming. In the kitchen of a small farmhouse outside the town of Chillicothe, the woman held the knife toward the growing crowd.

Mrs. Stephens was wearing a torn pink bunny nightshirt covered in blood. She was unmistakably pregnant, and unmistakably wounded, bleeding from wounds in her abdomen, self-inflicted wounds. "It's not his, so it's not mine. It don't count!" She reasoned hysterically, then fell to the floor.

Angie ran forward, took the knife out of the unconscious woman's hand, and attended to the wounds of the fallen pregnant woman. A few, including Martha, helped Angie, who seemed to be overwhelmed by the

God and Country

severity of the wounds. Most others waited in the living room. After about 20 minutes, Angie placed a table cloth over Mrs. Stephen's head and walked into the living room, shaking her head. Angie dropped to her knees, and began to weep uncontrollably and placed her head on Hunter.

"Her husband was killed," Angie muttered.

"I know, I was there. I'm so sorry," Hunter whispered in reply.

"I lost my husband," Angie buried her face in the shoulder of Hunter's injured arm.

Pain shot through Hunter's arm, making the irony of the moment even more poignant. He replied with the only reply possible. "I lost my wife."

Through tears, the two continued to hold each other, seemingly unable to let each other go.

Winter was very much upon the group, with the outside thermometer announcing three degrees above zero. Inside, the small stove was kicking out as much heat as it could. Two women were busy behind a makeshift blanket curtain, covering the door to the kitchen, mixing flour and water, making pancake batter. There was powdered milk, but it was reserved for the children. Two other women were in the living room, making pancakes on the stove top.

Hunter moved the tarp covering the front door and looked outside at the half-depleted woodpile on the front porch. "That isn't going to cut it," he thought, then smiled at the pun. For all that had been done to prepare for winter, there was still more left to do.

There was the water problem. There was none. The farmhouse had been built near the top of a hill, not exactly ideal for solving the water situation. There was an old cistern in the front yard, but it didn't hold water. There was a year-round stream at the bottom of the hill, but it was about 600 feet to the house. At first, a hummer was used to carry every water container the distance, but that was halted as people began seeing how scarce diesel was promising to be. This led to each couple or family carrying water for their own family. Water bottles were kept by each family. That was not an ideal solution, either.

Also, there was a problem sanitizing the water. On the second day staying at the farmhouse, it became evident that the water contained diarrhea-causing pathogens. A fire was kept burning even when there was no need for heat. Then, there were simply not enough containers to hold the purified water. There were a few occurrences of cross-contamination where people had used the same containers to both haul untreated water and store purified water.

Of course, diarrhea brought even more sanitary problems. Pedro and Martin, having found some tin and lumber in the shed, had constructed a trench latrine on the backside of the hill. A 5 gallon bucket was on the back porch, for emergencies. Still, it did not take much foresight to realize that there would be a devastating outbreak of illness soon.

A meeting of the group occurred in the living room to address the issues of heating and sanitation. Pedro, Melvin, and Mr. Evans were tasked with water purification and conveyance. Lola, Catalina, and Martha were tasked with sanitation, toiletry, and hygiene. Mr. Kaufman would still require shifts for both the observation posts and the security team. In addition, a scavenging and fuel team would be led by Hank, Hunter, and Martin to replenish the diminishing wood pile and find any other useful items. In short, the group would be kept busy.

As they broke off into teams, the purification team met on the back porch.

"That is 150 feet of vertical lift from the stream." Mr. Evans started, feeling overwhelmed. "The only way to lift that high is with a deep well pump. And we don't have a reliable source of electricity. We don't have the pipe nor connectors. What is next? Are we going to start another war just to go to the hardware store?"

Melvin had been listening, feeling the frustration of the young man he had trained for fifteen years. "Let's keep it simple. This place has a well, plumbing, and electrical connections. We simply do not have electric. Electricity is what we need and what we are trained for. Now, let's say that well house runs at about 700 watts. Start up wattage for the capacitor will be no more than three times that. We need a 2KW generator."

"But we don't have the fuel for that," Mr. Evans spoke up again.

"Let's not worry about what we don't have. Let's worry about what we need," Melvin said in response.

"We don't need electric all da time," Pedro offered up. "We can fill up a container, or we can plastic line that cistern."

A similar meeting occurred with the hygiene group. The problem was one of no soap.

"We have oil, these shortenings here, and we can make ash," Delores said matter-of-factly.

"You know how to make your own soap?" Martha asked.

"Oh, please, Martha. We washed and cooked lye as kids. Even when we came up here, I made extra money making soap and selling it on the internet to the gringos…umm, I mean you people."

"Oh, that would be simply amazing," Martha replied.
Martha and Lola laughed, but Catalina, Lola's sister, remained quiet.

"She misses her man," Lola confided to Martha when they found time alone.

"He died so we could all escape."

"I know, but that don't help Catalina none."

"We need to find a wind turbine," Hank told his brother.

"Yeah, and while we are at it, we can find a helicopter and just get out of here," Hunter countered.

"Actually, Melvin already knows where it is. A CAFO about fifteen miles from here."

"CAFO?"

"Confined Animal Feeding Operation. We are going to travel to a chicken farm!" Hank declared with a mocking enthusiasm.

The next morning, Melvin was accompanying Hank in a hummer. Behind them, another hummer was being driven by Martin, with Hunter

God and Country

manning the turret's M240 in the icy winter air. The wind was calm, but the hummer's speed put the freeze against Hunter's face. Using a scarf to offset the wind, Hunter cursed himself for not bringing goggles, or at least some glasses. Then there was the pain of his wound. Although Hunter's left arm ached, he still insisted on being as useful as possible. The frigid air gnawed at his knitting wound. Hunter's mind did not wander from his task, but in the back of his mind, he wondered about the event with Angie that occurred three days ago. More time for that later. He had a job to do.

"So what is the name of this place?" Hank asked the older passenger, as they were nearing their destination.

"Well, it really doesn't have a name of a town attached to it. People call that area Hawn's Mill, after the massacre," Melvin responded, nodding as if Hank understood the reference.

"Massacre?" Hank's mind thought of a great Native American tragedy, or perhaps the possible murder of African Americans that had occurred in Tulsa a hundred years ago.

"Mormons. Over 200 local people attacked the Mormons living there. They killed 17 men and boys. Drove them all out."

Hank tried to imagine the intolerance, the deaths of those who were only trying to live and defend their families. He could almost see the blood, smell the death.

Suddenly Hank realized that the death he was smelling was real. It reeked, reminding him of the church they had passed, by the North Bridge. Hank had smelled chicken farms before. They had a horrid smell all their own, but this smell was far worse than all others he remembered.

"The funnel houses lost power. No diesel, either. That is the smell of a hundred thousand dead birds." As they pulled up closer to the buildings, Hank glanced in the mirror to see his brother vomiting atop the hummer.

"Be glad it is not warmer."

The home, set off to the side, had been apparently abandoned. Hank understood why. Who could stand living here? The entire place was dead and smelled of death.

God and Country

"How did you know about this place, Melvin?" Hank asked.

"This place uses about 75 kilowatts per hour, and it is on our grid. How could I not know about it? Oh, and the only reason they bought this wind turbine was to serve as a tax write-off and to virtue signal how green they were. Maybe these chickens weren't free-range, but they were advertised as environmentally friendly."

According to Melvin, this place, along with most every outlying area, got cut when DHS dictated what areas could receive the limited power from the hydro. DHS received priority.

If the blackout had affected chickens this way, Hank didn't want to imagine what had happened at nursing homes and hospitals.

The four had no masks, and had to improvise using rags and paper. Hunter found some Pinesol, soaked some paper, and plugged his two nostrils, then used the rag as a mask. Even using his mouth to breathe through a disinfectant soaked rag, he was still retching.

The four found their prize: a 5 bladed turbine mounted at the crest of the ridge. Moving their hummers to that location, Melvin surveyed the situation quietly. The 24 volt battery array and inverter were still intact. How to drop the turbine was the question, a question that Melvin could not answer until he had assessed the situation. Which was what Melvin was doing right now.

"How are we going to get the windmill turbine down?" Hunter asked, as if it were the first time anyone had considered the question. "Are we going to climb up the top with a wrench?"

Melvin waited a bit longer, then walked in close to check the tower. "These mast sections disconnect. We take out one piece at a time, then use one of the guy wires as a rope to lower the pole down…slowly."

"You use the good ash, the white ash. Not any pine shit. Hard wood." Lola repeated the last words and then laughed a low chuckle. Lola had created a filter of small gravel and straw. She then began shoveling in the dead ash on the filter.

God and Country

"Plenty of ash means plenty of lye. More is better, right, Martha?" Lola, stopped shoveling to make a gesture requiring both hands. The gesture made Martha blush. Lola had two buckets, one full of water, one empty. "We pour da water on the top, and collect da lye on the bottom." Over the next hour, Lola emptied the lye back into the filter to continue the cycle.

"How do you know when the lye is ready?" Martha asked.

Lola smiled, her eyes lighting up behind her oversized 80s style sunglasses, and held out a feather. "When the lye eats this feather up, then it is good." Lola dipped the feather into the lye water, then withdrew it. The retrieved feather was singed with only a few vanes and part of the quill remaining. "This will burn you up like that feather."

Lola continued with an occasional lewd remark throughout the saponification process. The outdoor fire made for a bit more warmth, helping to warm the comparatively balmy thirty-five degree weather during that short December day. Catalina and Martha would alternate feeding the brick-enclosed fire, while Lola did what she was so good at, stirring the pot. That evening, Lola and Catalina were pouring the soap into molds constructed of 2x4 studs nailed to a piece of plywood. It would take a few days for the soap to set so they could cut it into bars.

—

Melvin had long discovered that the most difficult part of most tasks is acquiring the knowledge. The wind turbine had come down relatively easily, and the disassembling of the tower required only basic tools. Melvin smiled as he disassembled the 36 volt battery array and dual inverters. He had never assembled a wind generator system before, but he did know electricity very well. By the end of the day, the men had packed up their prize, lugging up the 6 12 volt batteries into the back of the hummer, as the temperature dropped with the setting sun.

Hank pulled the lead vehicle up to the front door of a metal building. He pulled open the door and discovered treasure. Not something as exciting as guns, nor food, but something just as necessary. Containers. Buckets. Heavy duty plastic. "Is that a welding kit?" Hank exclaimed.

God and Country

"We gotta make room for these two tanks." It was two days before Christmas, and at almost midnight, the "Windmill Expedition" arrived at their farmhouse homestead with all their treasures in tow. Hank felt like a very jolly Santa.

The next morning was Christmas Eve Day. Like every day, the guard outpost was to be manned. Six adults worked gathering and cutting wood, while others worked inside putting up heavy plastic in place of the badly needed extra blankets. Kaufman spent most of his time at the guard post, making the observation post virtually invisible from all around. Kaufman had somehow found an old railroad crank phone and had rigged up a permanent phone line back to the old dial phone in the kitchen. Melvin, Hank, and Pedro were working feverishly on the windmill, power supply, and pump house. There was to be no exchange of gifts, but that did not stop Hunter from cutting a small Christmas tree and returning it to the farmhouse. Hannah's eyes lit up when she saw the small cedar tree. "Daddy, I know just what we can do to decorate it!"

That Christmas Eve, everyone gathered in the living room where the Christmas tree stood in front of the window, opposite the wood stove. Hannah and four other children had adorned the tree with a box of Christmas ornaments. Red orbs of glass hung all over the tree. Gold icicles had been draped on the evergreen branches. There were even about two dozen Disney ornaments placed throughout the tree, with Mickey and Minnie ornaments staring at each other in the tree's center. Atop the tree was a beautiful white angel blowing a golden horn.

Hunter's and Angie's eyes caught each other while Martha was reading the Christmas story. Hunter suddenly realized why he had wanted to leave this place. He had been trying to run from his feelings. But he wasn't supposed to feel this way. Not yet. He looked back at Angie. Again, their eyes connected, then Angie looked away.

Martha continued with the Christmas story. *"...And when they were departed, behold, the angel of the Lord appeareth to Joseph in a dream, saying, Arise, and take the young child and his mother, and flee into Egypt, and be thou there until I bring thee word: for Herod will seek the young child to destroy him."*

That Christmas Eve night, Hunter's sleep was not one filled with visions of sugar plums, but of troublesome dreams. At the top of the hill, the farmhouse was on fire. He heard the voice of his mom calling him. *"Rise up,"* his mother warned. *"Flee into Egypt until I tell you."* Hunter looked up at the hill again, and there was Brittany, then suddenly, her face changed. It was Angie. The entire farmhouse then exploded, and Hunter awoke to the dawning Christmas morning.

Hunter got up and spent time at the wood stove. He had worked the coals of the hearth with tinder, twigs, and breath and was now appreciating the resulting flaming fingers of fire eagerly licking the edges of two well seasoned oak pieces. The fragments of his bad dream dispersed like the wood smoke drifting lazily outside over the bricked chimney. Hannah came into the living room, wrapped in her blanket. She pulled herself up beside her father and placed her head in his lap. Others began to arrive in the living room. Hunter turned his head toward the kitchen door…where Angie stood. She smiled. He smiled back, his dream long forgotten. For the Christmas Day meal, there was food aplenty. Bread stuffing, canned ham, instant potatoes, brown gravy, sweet potatoes, and homemade sourdough rolls.

Christmas had brought its own gifts: a sprinkling of snow, running water, and electricity. The 36 volt system had more than enough power for the well pump. Not only did the inverter and batteries power the pump, but there was enough electricity to power a breaker that ran the lights and wall outlets to the kitchen. "Just don't leave the lights on too long," Melvin chided the others, yet deep down Melvin felt a contentment he had not had in a while. Even now, his mind was racing as to where he could find a few solar panels.

Later that evening, Hunter found an opportunity to be with Angie alone.

"I should not feel this way, but I think about you a lot. I'm confused because I didn't want to feel this way. I can't help it," Hunter confided to her.

"I know, I feel it, too. But…"

Hunter knew what she was going to say. Angie was still married. No one knew what happened to Robert. He had been forgotten. But, not by Angie, not by Martha and Melvin, either. Something had to change. Something had to happen.

Chapter 8

Help

"What do you mean you are headed to town?" Hank questioned. At the same time he uttered the words, he realized he might know the answer already.

"We need to know where Robert is. We have to find out."

"Does this have something to do with you and Angie?" Hank had not been blind over the last two months. The two obviously had feelings for each other.

"And what if it does?"

"Look, Hunter. Slow down. Think of Hannah."

"I am thinking of Hannah. It is about her. It is about me. It is about our future." And, with that utterance, Hunter knew that it was about Angie. Without Angie, he had no future.

"And what if you find Robert? What then?"

"Then…I don't know what I will do…but Angie will be with her husband. And Martha and Melvin could be with their son-in-law."

"And if something happens to you, what about Hannah?"

"I've got to make a decision and take a chance somewhere. If I don't, why live at all? I want Angie to be with me. I need her to be with me. Damn it, I am betting my future on her, and I'm all in."

"So, you are going to look for Robert, so you can never be with Angie. That makes so much sense," Hank responded with bewildered sarcasm.

In some ways, the two brothers were total opposite. Hank could be quietly resolute. Hunter tended to be loudly bullheaded. However, once either one of them made up their mind, they were both adamant in their decisions.

"Okay, then. I'm going, too," Hank said quietly.

Hunter was not expecting this. He thought he hadn't heard his brother correctly.

"Huh?"

"I am going with you. You might be a dumb ass, but you are my brother. We started this journey together. We might end everything doing this, but we will do it together."

Nothing else was said as the two brothers embraced.

That evening the brothers met with Ron Kaufman. Kaufman, being a veteran of both the Iraq and Afghanistan wars, had displayed his wartime competencies in previous encounters.

"The Armory seems to be where DHS is holed up. They could have moved to the jail north of town. I had a peek at the town from the south side three days ago. It seems DHS was not able to keep the city in electricity. They are using diesel generators, most likely. Couldn't see the Armory from the edge of town. Of course, the jail is up Highway 65. Most likely, Robert is at the jail, if he is still...."

"We just need to know what happened to Robert. If he is still alive, we owe it to him to rescue him."

"The mission has two possible objectives. Are you prepared for both of them?" Kaufman waited for his inference to catch the two brothers. Silence answered the question.

"You want to come with?" Hank questioned.

"You need someone with tactical experience and knowledge of the area. I am your logical choice."

"The defense of the homestead depends in large part on you."

"The best defense is a good offense...if the situation calls for that. Besides, Robert got me my job. He gave me a second chance in life. Otherwise, I would still be in jail," Kaufman confided.

"You have been in this jail?" Hank began to seriously consider Kaufman's proposal.

"More times than I care to tell," Kaufman replied.

"Could you give us a good layout of the place?"

Kaufman did just that.

God and Country

The county jail consisted of a 64 cell four-pod design with an interior courtyard. South of the courtyard was the dining area. Beyond that was the parking area. North of the courtyard was a perimeter fence and a screening fence. The plan was to move by vehicle close to the river, then go on foot east along the river's edge, fording where possible. Afterwards, they would move north along the east edge of town and scout out the jail.

It was a late, moonless night, the second night of the new year, when Kaufman and the brothers moved out onto Highway 65. Hank creeped the blacked-out hummer down the road, while Hunter walked ahead marking the way with a red lens flashlight, acting more of a point man than a ground guide.

"There is no way we can break into that jail. Even with a dozen men," Hank commented to his veteran shotgun rider.

"I know that." Kaufman smiled, cradling an M240 machine gun, a generous belt of 7.62x39 mm ammunition draping over his neck. "I simply like being prepared," Kaufman responded wryly, a hint of amusement in his eyes.

Kaufman was obviously in his element. Indeed, he liked being prepared. Hank had spoken out against Kaufman taking the mortar system on the surveillance expedition, reasoning that it was the only means to keep the approach to the farmhouse properly defended. Kaufman, of all people knew that. Keeping Kaufman out of a fight, however, was going to prove difficult. Hank remembered Kaufman's "aggression" during the last raid, then thought of SSG Panning. Hank shuddered.

Hunter was walking point ahead of the hummer, trodding the half-frozen snow covered Highway 65 for almost two hours. His mind was confused; he knew that this expedition was his only hope to bring him some kind of peace. Was it wrong to hope that Angie's husband, Robert, was dead? Did he really believe that himself? What would happen if Robert came back? Hunter knew.

Hunter almost did not notice the slight bend in the road and the rise ahead that marked the descent into Chillicothe. He turned around, moved

God and Country

the red lens back and forth, then turned the light off. He walked thirty paces back to the hummer.

"I am going to recon the guard post a bit. We cross the river on the east side of the bridge."

"Yeah, but it's at least a half mile east," Kaufman responded.

"I want to follow the road by the tree line, then move east near the shore," Hunter proposed.

"We are all going," Hank responded, a bit of anger in his voice.

"Easy, big brother. I know that. We have the time right now, though, and I want to know for sure crossing here is not a mistake. I will be back." Hunter turned to leave.

"Here, take this." It was a small handheld two way radio. "Don't talk on it. Click once for radio check at the river. Click twice for us to follow. Three times rapidly means trouble."

Hunter nodded and left the vehicle, which pulled forward, then backed into a small opening among a group of cedar trees. He made his way through the woods over the crest of the hill.

Something was not right. Hunter was looking at the Highway 65 bridge. Where were the lights? The guard post was dark. The hydro station, the entire town, all dark. Hunter moved down the hill for a closer look, signaled a radio check, and studied the area, then studied some more.

"Hell, change of plans," Hunter whispered to himself. He had watched the guard shack for an hour and was convinced the guard post was abandoned. Better said, almost convinced. Hunter had made his way to the edge of the bridge. He picked up a fist-sized piece of limestone from the side of the bridge and hurled it toward the check point. The rock clattered a third of the way down the bridge. Hunter waited a moment, then began a weaving rush, from one concrete barrier to another, then paused again.

"Do I need a blindfold and a cigarette?" Hunter thought before he made the nervous walk across the middle section of the bridge, with a precarious feeling, as if he were walking the ice of a newly-frozen lake.

God and Country

Hank and Kaufman remained in the hummer parked inside the treeline. The cold had already crept into Hank's feet, and he occasionally stamped his feet to relieve the numbness. It also helped him relieve his frustration about not hearing from his brother. Then Kaufman cracked open his passenger door, stepped out, and leveled the deadly end of the machine gun toward the road waist-high.

Two bursts of radio static, quickly, came from the radio. Then another two bursts.

"Jesus," Kaufman exclaimed. "I almost wasted you."

"I didn't want you to take off through the woods and miss me," Hunter explained.

Hunter informed them about what he had discovered. "It seems totally dead. No lights at Winmart, none at the hotel."

"Well, it wasn't that way three days ago," Kaufman countered.

"Should we take the hummer across?" Hank offered.

"Hell, I walked across."

Moments later, their expedition continued, with Hunter walking ahead, M4 ready, and the hummer behind. Kaufman had mounted the M240 atop the gunner's well and was at ready, while Hank drove the blacked-out vehicle ahead. The vehicle traversed the staggered barricades of the bridge and passed the empty checkpoint. Hank looked east and west at the Highway 36 intersection where the two different fire fights had occurred. They kept moving ahead north along Main Street. The night was quiet, as would be expected at 4 a.m. There was, however, something ominous about the darkness. Kaufman was at ready, wide-eyed, warily manning the machine gun. Approaching the courthouse, Hunter walked by a plaque proclaiming something about being the home of sliced bread. He paused and listened. Nothing. Then Hunter continued, walking around the county courthouse and moving ahead, walking at a slow plod, with the vehicle following. He approached the National Guard Armory, raised a hand to the vehicle, and walked back.

"I am going to take a look," Hunter informed his brother.

God and Country

After a few minutes, Hunter returned. "All the vehicles are gone. The place was unlocked. They left quickly, it seems. There are papers and files scattered inside. One end of the parking lot has a pile of gear they left with no snow on it. They have not been gone too long. Kitchen equipment was left in the drill hall and some Mermites full of food. Veal." Hunter showed his other hand holding a breaded fillet. Hunter took a bite. "They left not long ago, and they were in a hurry."

"We need to go to the jail," Kaufman stated.

Hunter entered the back of the vehicle, and the hummer moved up the road at a somewhat faster pace. It turned right, and entered the jail parking lot. Again, there was no sign of life.

"I swear, they were just here a few days ago. Where the fuck are they?" Kaufman was livid. He had dismounted, machine gun in hand. He ran toward the front door. Locked. Not hesitating, Kaufman leveled a rather long burst of 7.62 mm rounds into the door, shattering the glass and chewing up the steel latch. The shots echoed in the stillness. As the echoes died, another noise replaced them. At first, Hank, who had made his way to the building, thought it was simply a ringing in his ears. Then he distinguished muffled cries, shouting.

"Back here," Hunter had made his way to the end of the hallway. Hunter opened the door to what was the dining facility. Hunter ran through the hall, out the back door, and to the first of the four inmate buildings. The front door was open. The shouting was louder now. Hunter entered the first building while Kaufman ran toward the other. The security room was open, but the last door was locked. A small ring of keys hung over a dead security panel. Hunter grabbed it and tried each key, fumbling from the panic and noise of crowds. He found the right key, opened the door, and was immediately hit by the stench of feces, urine and decomposition. Hank appeared behind Hunter, then ran back to the hummer. To hell with security protocol. They were going to need help.

In all, 527 citizens of Chillicothe had survived being confined in a facility designed for 128 inmates. Ninety-six had died. The prisoners, or better said, the survivors, were in an advanced state of malnourishment, having only eaten dry dog food for months. They had exited their cells as shivering, perambulating skeletons. What few blankets the mass carried with them were stinking rags of filth. They made their way to the dining hall. And, in the miserable, huddling crowd, Hunter recognized one of them. Robert.

Hank asked Robert to give as much information as he could about what had happened. "All I know is that on New Year's Eve, we heard trucks outside and some shuffling in the guard house. We were outside in the courtyard. The guards hurried us back inside, had us go to our cells, and locked us down." A pause then "…is Angie okay?"

After Robert had been captured, they had tried to get information from him, Robert went on to explain. He had been burned with a soldering iron on his inner thighs and privates.

"And you never told them about us?"

"How could I betray my Angie, my in-laws? No, not even when they did this." Robert raised up his hands, showing the unhealed scabs where his fingernails had been. Then he broke down in tears.

—

No one knew where DHS had gone. Some people had speculated that they had withdrawn toward Iowa. There were rumors that the commanding general of Fort Leonard Wood had defied the federal government's authority to help suppress the local population and had threatened government forces in the area. Others had suggested that a strategic redeployment of forces had occurred in Kansas City. Rumor had it that a rebellion had taken place west of Kansas City. Remarkably, a well-known member of the Kings baseball team, Aaron Bachman, had organized resistance to block and defend the I-70/I-435 exchange against government forces. There were all sorts of rumors flying around. A mutiny at Fort Knox. An outbreak of the bubonic plague in Florida. The rumor that interested Hank the most was one out of Oak Grove, Arkansas. That rumor involved a man named Hamilton. That was the last name of Hank's and Hunter's mom. And, that was where she lived.

Chapter 9

Broken

During the days that followed, Hunter had apparently lost interest in most things. He spent a lot of his time working, as did everyone, caring for the sick townsfolk, moving the last of the food from Winmart to the local hospital, and scavenging for antibiotics to fight the outbreak of dysentery that promised to plague the rescued townsfolk for months to come.

Out of necessity, the farmhouse was temporarily abandoned, and most of the hydro station workers lived near the hospital in houses that had been abandoned. Where over 8,000 people went remained a mystery. Following the initial incarceration of people living near the power station, the remaining population of Chillicothe seemed to melt away. There were occasional families that showed themselves near the courthouse, but apparently, regarding the issue of oppressive government occupation, the people of Chillicothe had voted with their feet.

The remaining residents of Chillicothe found themselves helping each other out of necessity. There was a healing in this. On the other hand, the brothers, Pedro, and his family found themselves lodging at the hotel south of town. Evenings for the brothers were a time when they helped maintain watch over the nearby intersection. It had been a very quiet time. Tonight, Hank had been thinking about his brother. When his brother arrived to relieve him, Hank spoke.

"You know, you were right. We helped these people. It was the right thing to do."

Hunter lightly sounded an affirmative in his throat.

Hank continued, "I do think, though, that we should talk about moving on." Hank used the equivocal term intentionally. Both of them stared at the moon in the clear southwest sky.

Hunter responded with another light groaning noise. Hunter felt like he was both lost and run over by a tank at the same time. Although Hannah had tried to talk with her father on several occasions, Hunter's

God and Country

response was the same monosyllabic, noncommittal response he had made to his brother now. Hunter half-listened to his older brother talk of crossing the Missouri River at Miami Station, move on through Versailles, and work their way across I-44. It meant nothing to Hunter. He had bet everything on Angie and had lost that bet. He seemed incapable of thinking about anything else.

Hank returned back to the hotel, leaving his brother to his watch duty. Lola's sister, Catalina, was in the lobby. Hank shook his head while Catalina poured him some coffee.

"Your brother is hurt," Catalina said softly. "Angie is, too. She takes care of Robert in the hospital. Angie says Robert is acting strange."

"How so?"

"I don't know," Catalina paused. Then she placed her hand on his. "You are a good man to take care of your brother."

"That's what brothers do."

"No, you are a good man. I see it. My husband was a good man." Tears appeared in Catalina's eyes. "I miss him."

"I know." Hank instinctively embraced her, and found in her embrace, a needed warmth.

The second week of January brought unusual weather. Vicious winds from the west were blowing through the town of Chillicothe. Lola had called this wind a "derecho." To Hank, it seemed like a tornado. Whatever it was, it blew the awning off the hotel entrance. Afterwards, a deep cold set over the town.

A small wood stove had been moved to room 103. The glass window had been removed to allow the stove pipe outside access. The lobby was used to store firewood and water. Blankets and mattresses covered the hallway entrances on the first floor blocking off 4 rooms. The two families stayed inside for the next three days as the temperature dropped to -20 degrees Fahrenheit. No watch was kept at the intersection. Instead a lookout was posted in the second floor stairwell. A two-way radio set communicated to room 103, and any problems could be reported to the hospital. Still, anyone venturing out in that cold was going to be badly hurting. It was unlikely that anyone would be traveling in that weather. At least that's what everyone was thinking, until Hunter got on the radio from his watch station. "We have an 8 ton military vehicle crossing the 65 bridge heading north. Moving slowly." Hank answered an acknowledgement, and relayed the message to the courthouse checkpoint. Then, Hank and Pedro ran out to the hummer. Hank hit the glow plugs, waited, then attempted to start the vehicle. The vehicle motor turned over, but didn't start.

"Shit," Hank muttered under his breath. Hank then hit the glow plugs a second time, turned the motor over, and to his relief, the motor started.

Pedro had placed the M240 on the turret mount. He adjusted his pile cap, wrapping down the cheek pieces more firmly. He put on a second stocking cap as Hank took off. The bitter cold bit at Pedro's face. About 200 yards ahead, the larger vehicle surged past Hank's hummer, crossing the intersection, attempting to gain speed. This would prove to be a mistake. Hank carefully drove his vehicle. He knew from experience that 4 wheel drive could only perform so well on solid ice. When the 8 ton drove past, accelerating, in an apparent attempt to evade him, Hank smiled and thought to himself, "Go right ahead, fuckers."

As Hank followed at a distance, the large vehicle approached the town square. Being forewarned, Kaufman had disconnected a prepositioned semi trailer which rolled across the road, and had crashed against a parked Ford F150. Kaufman had also prepositioned the Ford truck. He smiled as the large barricade crashed against the truck, stopping.

"Best use for a Ford," Kaufman muttered.

Kaufman saw the approaching 8 ton vehicle and knew from the speed that the vehicle was not stopping, could not stop. Three men in the cab of the truck realized their fate as the truck skidded toward the obstacle ahead. They were wearing blue helmets.

"U.N." Kaufman snarled as the inevitable crash occurred. Those helmets spared the driver and door passenger from head injuries, but did

God and Country

not prevent their necks from snapping as the vehicle went from 40 mph to zero in an impactful instant. The middle passenger, who managed to survive the impact with only a few broken ribs and facial injuries, succumbed to the violent entry of a 9mm round into his face, discharged from Kaufman's pistol. Kaufman ran to the back of the vehicle, a maniacally-crazed grin on his face, and would have dispatched the passengers in the rear as well had Pedro not fired a burst from his M240. Hank pulled over, got out, and yelled, "Kaufman, you okay?"

Kaufman just smiled that empty smile again.

"Kaufman!" Hank yelled again, walking up to him. Kaufman slumped his shoulders.

"I got carried away, huh?"

"Yeah, ya did," Hank paused. "Good job!" Hank put his hand on the shoulder of the troubled man. Hank realized that in normal times, Ron Kaufman should never be anywhere near a loaded gun. These were not, however, normal times, and sometimes having the biggest mad dog in the fight was the safer option.

There were eight surviving United Nation personnel in the rear of the crashed military vehicle. Another four had succumbed to gunshot wounds. The soldiers were disarmed, searched, and segregated in the local jail north of town. Their arms and ammunition would be distributed to the most healthy of the townsfolk, a growing number now that the 600 townsfolk had been fed a more nutritious diet, yet the problem of a diminishing food supply loomed large overhead.

Hank, Kaufman, and Melvin had driven up to the jail to question the UN prisoners. They were greeted by some of the townsfolk that had been rescued from the jail some 15 days before. One townsperson, a pale, dark haired woman with a large rose tattoo behind her ear, held up a gaunt hand in a half wave, half instruction. Hank stopped the vehicle.

"Are all prisoners available for questioning?"

"Seven of them are. One tried to escape so we had to shoot him…in both knees. He bled out about half an hour ago." The woman gave a wry smile, one that Hank didn't return. He simply tightened his lips and nodded his head.

"Jesus," Hank thought, "In three days there will be no prisoners left." This concerned Hank, both morally and pragmatically, because he needed answers.

Hank and Melvin, who seemed to have become the informal leader of the town, had talked about the necessity of the interrogation. Although the town of Chillicothe had no beef with the federal government, the townsfolk had been looted, imprisoned, starved, raped, tortured, and killed. The conflict was not political. It was personal. There would be two points of focus to the interrogation: What was the enemy threat to the town, and what were possible sources of food and supplies.

A single guard moved to the door of the cell block. Hank questioned as to why the guard had a handkerchief over his nose. When the door opened, Hank realized that the rank odor of feces, urine, and decay had not been purged. His nose wrinkled.

"Yeah, we haven't cleaned this one yet," the guard confessed. "Just seemed right to put them here."

The UN prisoners had been assigned separate cells. The guard opened the first cell. Inside, on the heavily painted board that passed as a cot, the prisoner had sat. When Hank, Kaufman, and Melvin entered the cell, he stood up silently. He wore the insignia of what appeared to be a higher ranked sergeant.

"French," Kaufman muttered in disgust.

"Oui," responded the prisoner. "First Sergeant Pierre Leblanc of the United Nations North American Response Force, and I demand to speak to the person in charge regarding our brutal treatment and unhygienic quarters." The prisoner spoke quite fluently although with a heavy French accent. There was an air of superiority in his eyes in spite of his current circumstance.

"Let's go somewhere where we can talk," Hank nodded toward the door.

God and Country

They left the cell where Leblanc had been held, exited through the guard entrance, and walked across the courtyard where the wind whipped wildly, blowing a chill into their bones. They entered the dining facility and sat at a long folding table.

"We will look into your conditions and see what we can do," Melvin started. His gray hair and mustache complimented his deep voice, adding to his evident authority. Hell, Hank thought, Melvin was indeed in charge. Hank held his peace and listened further to Melvin as he continued.

"Why are you here in Missouri? Who sent you here?" Melvin inquired firmly.

"I need not explain myself. Certainly you understand that, as a soldier, I cannot give information regarding my mission." Leblanc countered.

"I am trying to understand who you are. You complain about your captivity? That is where my friends and family were held. The smell of shit and piss? That is where they were crammed seven people to a cell designed to hold two. The rotten smell? That is the bodies of my lifelong friends who died here. So, yeah, we will look into these conditions you protest. But first, you contemplate what we have been through."

"Now," Melvin's eyes narrowed. "You need to explain why you are in our town. I am listening."

Leblanc quietly considered Melvin's words and then began to speak. "Our response force was invited here by your president. Your president said this was a mission to preserve democracy, to preserve liberty."

"The people of my town were oppressed, forced out of their homes, imprisoned, killed. Does that sound like your idea of fucking liberty?" Melvin responded. He had not raised his voice in the least, but it was evident from the tone of his voice and the fire in his eyes that Melvin was angry.

"Where can I find food for my town? Does that run counter to your idea of liberty, feeding people?"

"There is a camp outside St. Louis. We send people there."

God and Country

"You send people there?"

"Oui," Leblanc almost whispered.

"Why did you come to Chillicothe? What happened to your men?"

"We were retreating to your city of Des Moines. Some of your army are in rebellion against your United States."

"Where is the rebellion?"

Leblanc spoke the words slowly in his heavy French accent. "Leonard Wood."

"Will there be more of you coming?"

Leblanc remained quiet, realizing he had spoken too much, but his silence spoke volumes.

—

Robert was slowly recovering, physically. His injured fingers and genitals were responding well to the antibiotics, although he had lost his right testicle. It was not necessary for someone to tell Robert he had been rendered sterile. A constant aching pain reminded him. Angie and he had tried unsuccessfully for several years to have a child, and they had taken this from him now. Anger overtook him at times. The only reason that Robert had continued to live was his love for Angie. Out of necessity, Angie had become an obsession. Now, Robert was with her again, but somehow, Angie seemed different. She loved him, so she said, but compared to his love, hers seemed an indifference.

The couple had moved to an abandoned home near the hospital, the Miller residence. No one knew where the Millers had gone, but conventions regarding abandoned property had changed. The Miller place had a wood stove in the living room, which was a necessity in this harsh winter.

Robert was in the backyard. The shed there had rendered a decent supply of lumber for fuel. It hurt Robert's hands using the ax, but for some reason the biting pain combined with the numbing cold seemed to console him, dulling the pain he felt as he thought of Angie. She didn't love him. She could smile at him, kiss him, make love to him, but Angie did not love

God and Country

him like Robert loved her. Or was he growing mad? Robert couldn't tell. Something was not right.

———

Angie was going through the empty houses on her block. Most houses had been looted for food, but she had been able to find useful items. She tried to keep her mind focused on the task at hand and not to think of his name, otherwise the feelings would overwhelm her again. She had made her choice. What choice was there really? She was married. She would get past this; no, they would get past this together. Robert was still acting strangely. Was it because he knew something was wrong?

"Just focus. One foot in front of another," Angie thought to herself. "Keep moving forward." Another tea kettle, good find. She walked outside and placed it in the toy wagon. Another house yielded 4 blankets and three cans of cat food. A different house search brought two bottles of aspirin, a bottle of ibuprofen, and a prescription of ampicillin. She could keep some of the meds for her husband, Angie thought, and take the rest down to the hospital. It was a game to play to keep her mind off things. In the basement of another house, Angie found a car emergency kit containing three road flares and a case of unused mason jars. Treasures? Sure, why not? Angie smiled.

It was getting late and the light from the bleak sky did not penetrate the high windows of the basement very well. Angie lit a candle. She noticed something in the corner. A bowling ball bag. "Well, I guess we could go bowling when things get back to normal…IF we get back to normal." Angie's smile disappeared and she almost forgot about the bag, then reached for it. Empty, no, not empty. Something was inside. Angie unzipped the bag, reached inside, and felt something recognizable: a gun. Angie pulled out the snub-nosed revolver and a box of .38 ammunition. Angie tucked the small gun in her jacket pocket. She felt more comfortable carrying the pistol, but didn't know why. Angie went back outside and returned to the house with her find. Was it home? No. But perhaps one day it would feel like home.

———

God and Country

"How is our fuel?" Hank asked?

"We have a barrel of gasoline scavenged from vehicles. The four hummers have been topped off. We have pulled the tanker back to the armory." Hunter responded.

"Additional vehicles?"

"Twelve trucks. 5 diesel, the rest gas, all topped off." Trucks had been deemed a more valuable asset due to their extra hauling capacity.

"Arms?"

"We gained 12 rifles." Kaufman responded, passing a rifle to Hank. It was a bullpup rifle, with the magazine well set behind the trigger.

"Called a FAMAS 3." Kaufman remarked. "Pretty easy to operate. Besides that, 3 Berettas, and a machine gun. They are French but are NATO standard. The machine gun, a MAG 58, has 8 belts that fit our M240."

"So, all together, 34 assault rifles, 6 pistols, 2 machine guns, and one mortar system to defend a town? That isn't a lot."

"You forgot the M203, grenades, and a couple of shotguns. But you are correct. Not a lot," Kaufman admitted. "I would recommend a defense of 65, extending the slalom after the bridge up the hill. We can use the slowed approach as a capture or kill zone with machine gun and mortar support. We close other roads, and a proactive patrol that can be opportunistic. Split our assets in two. One defensive, one offensive. Best defense is a…"

"Good offense. I'm following you." Hunter said, nodding.

"How can we close down the other roads?" Hank asked.

"Use the trees. We fall them along the roads. Use uphill to our advantage. On the hill east of town, we can create a very effective barrier. Since we need some avenues of regress, we might be able to leave open Iris Road and AA."

"Pedro, how many people are available for this?" Hank asked.

Pedro responded, "Maybe 70 of the townspeople can work or carry a weapon. Dysentery, infected wounds, malnutrition, mental health. Some people do not need to be carrying a weapon."

God and Country

Hank glanced quickly at Kaufman with that last statement. Kaufman was a demonstrated expert in battle tactics, but it was obvious he could be a *bit* unstable.

―

Angie was becoming more worried about her husband. Upon her return from scavenging, she found Robert kneeling in front of the wood stove, blowing on the coals to ignite the 2x4 planks he had broken up. A quarter rick of cut lumber was stacked in the living room near the stove; the ax he had used leaned up against it. Angie came in the house carrying the tea kettle. Robert looked over his shoulder and smiled a toothy, exaggerated grin. A chill ran down Angie's spine.

The rest of the night, Robert was quiet, despite Angie's efforts to strike a conversation. In bed, Robert remained eerily quiet. Angie realized he was not sleeping, so Angie didn't sleep that night either…

The next morning Angie stated, "Honey, I need to get these meds and blankets to the hospital. I left some on the counter for you. Moxi and Advil."

"Oh, really? What time should I expect you back?"

"It shouldn't take very long unless they need help."

"It won't take very long unless…needs help," Robert thought to himself.

"Have fun." Robert came over and gave his wife an overelaborate kiss, then an almost maniacal grin.

"Okay." Angie breathed a sigh of relief as she left the house, not noticing the living room curtain pull back slightly behind her.

The hospital indeed needed help. Angie spent the next three hours changing bandages and soiled bedding. Then she went down to see if the kitchen needed help.

Lola and Catalina were in the makeshift outdoor kitchen, making flatbread on a sheet of iron at least six feet long.

Mr. Evans was employed full time feeding the improvised brick stove underneath the huge griddle. Mrs. Fletcher and three other women carried bread back to a table and tended two huge containers fashioned out of 30 gallon steel barrels.

"Beans, tortillas, and cornbread. We take the corn, white corn, flour, don't matter. We make the bread. Come here. You can help, but wash your hands first, hun." Lola took Angie by the hand to a wash basin, and then led her to her own space.

"We could only make six at a time. Otherwise they burnt. Now we can rock." Lola smiled a wicked smile, rocking her hips quite expertly.

Angie's lack of skill quickly demoted her to mixing and ladling out cornmeal patties. Canned corn and green beans were added to the mixture, although sparingly, as vegetables were in short supply. Actually, everything was in short supply. Here at the hospital, the remaining food from the Winmart supply was being rationed out. Rations consisted of rice, beans, and flour as staples. plus anything extra that could be rounded up.

Angie was so busy pouring cornbread that she almost missed Hunter at the table, coming in for a late lunch. She finished pouring the batch of cornmeal, then made her way over to the serving table.

"I never got a chance to thank you for finding Robert," Angie said in a sad way.

"I did it for me."

"What do you mean?"

"I had to know. I guess you had to know, too. Now we know."

Hunter gestured with his hands, then placed them on the narrow table. Angie moved her hands atop his, in a futile attempt to offer Hunter some comfort.

"I'm sorry. I had to choose. I love you, but he is my husband. I couldn't leave him."

"I know."

Unknown to both of them, Robert was observing the scene from behind a rusted yellow backhoe across the street. Finally, he knew what was going on. Robert walked forward. He knew what must be done. In his hand, he held his father's shotgun.

"I knew it! I knew something was going on," Robert yelled, narrowing the distance between him and the field kitchen, his leveled shotgun leading the way.

"I loved you! How could you do this to me? Betray me like this? I went through hell for you! Hell! You slut!" Robert aimed the shotgun at Angie.

"Robert, please! Nothing happened! I still love you. Put the shotgun down!" Angie pleaded through tears.

Robert shifted his weapon toward Hunter. "How could you do this to me? You abandoned me so you could fuck my wife? You piece of shit!"

"For God sake, Robert! He rescued you! He saved our lives!"

Robert raised his shotgun to shoulder level and aimed it at Hunter. "Today, you go to hell…I am already there."

Suddenly, there were three shots in rapid succession. Robert staggered, then fired the shotgun. The blast rang through the air as Robert fell.

Angie stood, revolver in hand. Then she dropped the gun and ran to her dying husband. Cold breaths of steam came from Robert's mouth as blood began to appear from his jacket.

"Oh, God, Robert, I am so sorry."

"I love you, Angie," Robert softly whispered, blood coming from the edge of his mouth. His eyes fixed, as if on something distant, one last time.

"I love you, too, Robert," Angie whispered, then began to weep, quietly at first, then more loudly, embracing her husband's lifeless body.

"Oh, God! What did I do?…Why?"

Hank and Pedro were walking toward the hospital when they heard the shots. Quickly closing the three blocks from the courthouse, the two arrived at the parking lot. Angie was still lying on her husband, crying softly. Hank walked over to his brother, who still seemed speechless over what had just happened.

"What the hell happened?"

God and Country

"Robert was going to shoot her, was going to shoot me....Angie shot him."

After the two brothers talked, Hank went over to Angie. He put his hand on her shoulder. Angie looked up at Hank, then pushed his hand away.

"No, go away. Please."

Hank backed away. An old black Chevy Silverado pulled into the parking lot. The door opened, and Melvin got out. He ran over to his dead son-in-law. Angie embraced her father. A few minutes later, Melvin got up and walked over to the two brothers. His eyes contained sorrow and anger.

"Why did you bring my son-in-law back? Was it just to kill him?" Melvin asked, as his eyes filled with tears.

"I didn't do anything. We didn't..." Hunter said, not knowing how to explain.

"I don't care, damnit! Melvin shouted in fury, then got control of himself. "I can't see straight right now. I need time."

Hank responded, "I am so sorry. Robert wasn't well."

"I know. We just need some time to process this."

Chapter 10

Goodbyes

The two brothers left with Pedro, walking silently back toward the courthouse. Pedro was the first to begin speaking.

"Melvin is hurt."

"I hurt him," Hunter responded.

"You didn't," his brother interjected.

"Bull shit. I fucked it up."

"I saw everything, didn't I? You did everything right. Sometimes life is fucked up."

Hunter looked at his brother and half-whispered, "Then why do all the fuck-ups seem to happen around me?"

"It will get better. Give them time to grieve," Pedro offered.

The three got into their hummer and drove toward the hotel.

Later that evening, the brothers sat in front of Room 102's wood stove. The glass door of the small wood stove helped glowing coals radiate throughout the room, but it could do little to move heat to the other three icy rooms they had partitioned off from the rest of the hotel. As a result, Pedro, Lola, and Catalina were in the room as well. The brothers continued their discussion about their future in Chillicothe.

"We need to move on. The townsfolk here will make it or they won't. What we do will neither add nor take away from that," Hank said quietly.

Hunter simply nodded. There was no way he could clear his head, but he could use some space. Hannah remained quiet, her head on her father's lap.

Pedro joined in: "Catalina, Lola, and I want to go with you. We have friends in northwest Arkansas. You are going there, no?"

"No, actually we are planning to go the other way. Headed Southeast toward the other side of the state."

God and Country

"Oh." A lengthy conversation developed between Pedro, Lola, and Catalina in their native tongue.

The brothers spent the rest of the evening packing their belongings in the hummer. The M240 machine gun would stay with the town. The brothers would take the four rifles brought with them, 2 cases of ammunition, a few fragmentation grenades, and what passed as an adequate supply of dry goods, cooking supplies, and shelter needs.

The next morning, two brothers and one little girl stood in front of the hotel. The late January sun rose to a clear morning. Maybe it was freezing now, but it would warm later. The hummer emitted its diesel fumes in a metered puffing out the back.

Pedro, Lola, and Catalina emerged from the lobby. Catalina held two bags with her. The three approached the hummer. "We will miss you, Hunter." Pedro shook Hunter's hand. Lola hugged him.

"Hank, you are a good man," Hank and Pedro shook hands.

"Goodbye, Lola," Hank smiled at her.

Lola hugged him and whispered, "Catalina has something to say to you."

Catalina stood apart from the others. She walked up to Hank and started: "I want to go with you, Hank. Wherever you go, I want to be with you."

It was a blunt statement of fact, one that took Hank by surprise, not by her desire, but by its directness. And with that surprise, came an awareness to Hank. He wanted her to be with him as well.

The four left the hotel, on their way to the courthouse. About 6 blocks from their destination, Hunter slowly stopped the vehicle. Ahead, an old black Silverado slowed and stopped. Melvin and Angie exited the truck. Hank and Hunter got out of their vehicle as well.

"Going somewhere?" Melvin began.

"Just wanted to tell you that we are headed out. Pedro has the weapons and inventory at the hotel." Hank responded.

"Look, Robert wasn't right. I knew that. I was just hurting. You've done so much. You don't need to go."

"Thank you, Melvin, but we do need to go. You have your town to look after. We need to be with our family."

Angie and Hunter had moved off.

"Hunter, I am so confused."

"I know."

"No, you don't. You see. When Robert came back to me, when you brought him back, I had to stay with him; I had to love him. He was my husband. But I never stopped loving you. God knows I tried. I fought it. But you were always there!" Angie smiled through tears, reaching out to touch Hunter's face.

"Yeah, I tend to get that response from people," Hunter offered, smiling back.

"Yes, you do. Damn it. Yes, you do. You can't just leave me here."

Leaving Chillicothe was no easy task. Melvin insisted that the brothers stay the day. "What were you planning to do? Leave during the daytime? Hell, everyone's leaving." The old man expressed a sad, wry smile under eyes near tears. Melvin recovered. "Get some lunch. Then we will try to come up with some sort of plan for you to go south."

Melvin had been through a lot, Hank thought. Hank couldn't imagine how Melvin felt. His son-in-law was dead. His daughter was leaving as well.

That afternoon, Kaufman and Melvin studied county maps from the courthouse.

"No sign of DHS in Carrolton, but that won't do you any good. The bridge south of there is occupied. Seems DHS and NATO find it easier to hold I70 if you hold access across the river."

"Miami?"

"Same thing. The truth is that the bridges are occupied all east up to St. Louis. I doubt you would have better luck crossing the Mississippi," Kaufman quipped.

"How in the hell do we go south?" Hunter began feeling frustrated.

"Well, you could consider going west. Can't promise anything, but it seems that that baseball player, Bachman, has managed to create quite the groundswell movement east of KC. I don't know how popular you would be showing up in a DHS hummer, though. He has shut down the KC Southern Railroad going east to St. Louis.

"Damn, he was a good left fielder. Loved him." Hunter, like his mom, was an avid Kings fan.

"Seems like most people in KC do as well."

That evening, a loaded-down hummer with five occupants crossed the 65 bridge south of town. The two brothers said their goodbyes to Kaufman, who warned them about the mortar mine traps at the end of the bridge. "Just keep to the left on your way out. I will walk you out. Hate to waste a good mortar on ya!"

"Love you, man." Hunter responded.

"I want to go with you, but I know my place is here."

"I know." Hunter moved the hummer forward up the hill on 65.

Ten minutes later, the vehicle went past the gravel road that led to the farmhouse. It was a reminder of all that had occurred in the last three months. The hardships and peril seemed to produce the deepest friendships, Hunter mused to himself. He looked over to see Angie riding shotgun, smiling back at him. They drove on.

Driving in blackout drive, they turned west on Highway 10. There was, occasionally, a faint haze of light glowing in the south at the horizon.

"What do you think?" Hunter asked over his shoulder.

Hank manipulated the state map of Missouri and a military-issue red lens flashlight.

"This is the one. We follow this. Ever drive down railroad tracks before?"

"Not while sober," Hunter grinned, then turned the hummer south onto the raised railroad tracks.

Hank got out and started walking ahead, scarcely able to see much in the dark, moonless, cloudy night. Hunter drove the hummer close behind him, concentrating on the glowing cat-eyed band that Hank had circled his hat, careful to maintain the straddle of the railroad tracks. The railroad bed was slowly rising higher than the farmland around it as they

God and Country

traveled, making Hunter painfully aware of how vulnerable they were. Only the dark night added a certain security, and mystery.

Hank approached the bridge. There was no turning back now. Actually, there had not been for some time. Although it was difficult to determine distance, Hank knew that there was a little over a mile before the hummer could get off the tracks. He only hoped that the trains were not up and running again. Hank stepped on the wooden cross tie and could feel the light breeze coming up under his feet. He placed a foot forward, feeling the gap. About 5 inches between ties. Maybe more. Hank took another step. And another. The pedestrian walkway, about 6 feet to his left, was a tempting yet impossible option, for Hank had to provide the only guide for his brother, who was navigating the large vehicle across the river with only about a foot and a half clearance on each side.

The air blew up from under the bridge and tickled Hank's face as he realized it was beginning to snow. Small flakes mean big snow, Hank thought, more than halfway across the river. It was cold enough without the snow. They needed to take shelter. Hank strained his eyes to the opposite shore. It was incredible how much distance they had traveled this evening, eighty miles, but it was in the opposite direction. Was it a mistake to leave in the fall? No one would have ever suspected it would have taken three months to make this journey. How would they ever get to Oak Grove?

The wind howled again, louder. Wait, Hank thought. Then again. Hank turned around toward the vehicle immediately behind him and waved his red light.

"Train!" Hank screamed.

"Jesus," Hunter responded.

Hank ran back to the vehicle. "Fuck this." Hank hopped in the back seat. Hannah, who had been asleep in the back, woke up.

"Turn on your lights and go!"

Hunter complied, accelerated the hummer.

"What is wrong, Daddy?"

God and Country

"Oh, nothing, baby girl." Hunter turned around a second and smiled. "Just having fun." Hunter looked at the distant light in front of him.

"Okay, we made it across. Turn off!"

"This is still a bridge! I got to keep going."

"Find a place to turn."

"Buckle up! Gonna be rough!" Hunter yelled then started talking to himself, yelling at himself, reliving some episode from his past. "Gotta drive toward a damned train. I said 'never again.' Swore it!"

The bumpy ride along cross ties turned into a rumbling roar. The train was closer now, its light began to brighten inside the hummer. The train blasted its horn in seeming inevitability.

"There!" A steep embankment had replaced the railroad tie bridge.

The train blasted again, terribly close.

Hunter turned the wheel. Was it too late? The train screamed by, and Angie screamed as well, as the hummer left the tracks, jumping the embankment. The roaring train decreased in volume. The vehicle hit the limestone gravel with an impactful thud and continued its descent. Hunter instinctively moved his hands to the wheel, fighting to regain control of the vehicle. The hummer hurled straight down the embankment moving toward a grove of willows at the bottom.

"Oh shit!" Hunter uttered then came the rushing sound of moving past leaves. Another jump through the air. A thud. Hunter again regained control of the vehicle and hit the brakes. The vehicle skidded to a stop in front of a large pile of white rocks. He looked over at Angie.

"You okay?" Hunter asked Angie. Angie nodded quietly, stunned. Hunter turned around.

"How about you, kid?"

"Uhhh," Hannah replied, looking at her father concerned.

"Catalina?"

"I'm okay."

"Hank?"

"I'm good, man."

God and Country

"You got blood coming from your forehead," Hunter observed.

"Damned rifle got me," Hank responded. "Hell, have you looked in a mirror?"

Hunter lowered the window and looked at his rearview mirror, adjusting it. His forehead had a gash. Hunter was sure it was a bad cut. He touched under his lower lip. He felt blood and something hard. He had lost a tooth.

Hunter shut off the lights and engine and stepped out of the vehicle. The train had not stopped and was across the river. The hummer, like him, was okay. Just a little frontal damage was all. Then, Hunter staggered and collapsed.

Chapter 11

Trust

Angie sat there looking at Hunter, who was lying on the floor in a small shed at the quarry where they had crashed. Hunter had been unconscious for almost two hours. She wasn't much of the praying kind, but it was becoming more and more clear that they needed all the help they could get. As she fumbled in her prayer, Angie stopped suddenly. What was she to call Hunter? I mean, they were not married. Until yesterday, she had been married to Robert, who she had thought to have been dead until two weeks ago. Was Hunter her boyfriend? No, theirs was a lifelong commitment. Hunter was definitely her man. Forever.

"Dear Lord, I don't know what to say. I just ask that you look out for Hunter and protect…"

Angie was interrupted by a noise from the outside. It sounded like vehicles. She got up, opened the door and, by early morning light, walked around the building to see what was going on. Hank, Catalina, and Hannah had their hands up and were being searched by a group of 6 soldiers. Hannah looked Angie's way, and Angie could see the terrified look in the little girl's eyes. Hank said something to Hannah, but it was too late. The soldiers had noticed Angie. One of them yelled at her, ordering her to come there. Angie walked slowly over, comprehending what was occurring. She was roughly searched.

Hannah started to cry. "But, what about Daddy?" she questioned Hank.

The soldiers searching them apparently did not hear the little girl. They finished the frisking of their prisoners. "You are now being detained for further questioning."

"By whose authority?" Hank questioned the flinty-eyed sergeant.

"Vice-President Clinton," came the rote response.

God and Country

Vice-President Clinton? Hank had never paid attention to the news, but any news in this upside-down world was noteworthy. That Vice President Biden had not managed to succeed as president was not surprising; Biden was a politician, not a leader. Hank quickly threw the thought from his mind, gathered himself, and continued. "Why are you detaining us?"

"For this." The sergeant held up an M4.

Hank wondered why the seemingly very competent sergeant had not checked behind the utility shed, where he would find quite a bit more of this "contraband." Instead, he simply nodded, hoping somehow that the soldiers would not look any further. And somehow, that was exactly what happened. The sergeant loaded his four prisoners into the back of his vehicle and drove away from the quarry.

―

Hunter woke up groggily. When he rose to get up, he became suddenly dizzy and nauseous. It felt as if an ocean sloshed in his head, and its echo continued. Hunter placed his head back down slowly, waiting for the waves to stop. "Yeah, that is going to be a problem," Hunter thought. Hunter slowly placed his hand on his forehead to feel his gash and a large lump that seemed to pulse. Hunter closed his eyes and tried to let the pain subside.

―

Catalina looked at Hank, fear in her eyes as the two hummers pulled into the entrance of what appeared to be a large concrete parking garage built into the side of a mountain. The hummers pulled into the entrance and in to darkness.

―

Hunter awoke a second time, and this time he managed to raise himself, however not without the dizzy sloshing. Where was everyone? He looked around the room. It appeared to be a small shed. He had been laying on his and Angie's coat, but where was Angie? Hunter steadied himself against a metal stud and slowly raised himself. Could he make it? Yes, he could. Slowly, carefully, he made his way to the door. He pushed the door open, it swung wide and bright: bright light. Hunter collapsed again in the doorway, passing out yet again.

When Hunter awoke, he found himself still in the shed, covered with what appeared to be a tent canvas. Underneath him was something rolled up, soft, like a quilt. In front of him, an old man sat next to a compact camp stove, heating up some water.

"Raman noodle," the old man said in a severe southern drawl. The man looked as if he had traveled quite a while. The leather of his boots were scuffed and a bit torn. He wore an old army field jacket, the several tears of its canvas carefully mended with thread that did not match the olive drab material. Hunter was reminded of the jacket from that famous old movie about the Vietnam veteran. Maybe the old man was a Vietnam vet. A year before, society would have instantly labeled the old man homeless. At least at first. Upon careful observation, however, the man's appearance told a different story. Although his clothes were old and dirty, he himself appeared well groomed. His hair was grayed, well-kempt. His hands were calloused but clean. Behind a neatly trimmed beard, the old man's face appeared to have seen more than his share of experience. There was a certain wisdom in the old man's eyes. Remarkable. And when he continued to speak, that entire refined image was irretrievably lost.

"That there is my own special recipe. It should help you with that goose egg on your head." Hunter tried not to laugh as he heard the word "head" pronounced with two distinct syllables. Suppressing that laughter, however, was easy enough. The pressure to his head was making him nauseous as it was.

Hunter closed his eyes again. He heard a spoon stirring as it hit against the old tin cup. It seemed the stirring continued for a long while, almost lulling him back to sleep. Then the spoon made a muted rap-rap against the side of the tin, announcing the completion of the concoction.

"Here ya go."

The man pushed up a blanket behind Hunter's back, offering Hunter some support as he raised up. As promised, it was a cup of Rama Noodles, with some extra herbs floating at the top.

"Can't eat much, probably, but the secret is in the sauce," the old man said.

Hunter gave a slight nod, and sipped. "Not bad," Hunter remarked to himself.

"You learn how to create good things out of next to nothing when you have been around as long as I have."

"Where is my daughter, my brother…" Hunter paused, not knowing how to finish the sentence.

"The two women you have been traveling with?"

"Yes. Where are they?"

"The government done took them away. I was sitting underneath that there willow tree and saw the whole thing."

"What? Huh? Why didn't they take me?" Hunter was confused.

"Who knows. The Lord works in mysterious ways."

"Who are you?"

The old man placed his hand on Hunter's shoulder and smiled.

"Call me Jesse. I'm a friend. Right now it seemin' I'm the only friend you got." The old man smiled. "Guess I am playin' like a doctor for now."

"I've got to find my…"

"Your family." It was more of a statement than a question. "Yeah. I reckon you do. You need mending, though. Seems you got to get your head workin' right."

Jesse was correct, but Hunter's mind could not help racing. How would he find his family? Hunter took another sip of the salty, chicken-flavored noodles. It was good. He again took a deep draw of the soup.

"Good, huh? Tole ya. I've been told I make a mean soup."

Hunter's head was getting clearer. He began to get up.

"What you need right now, son, is to rest," the old man said. "You can't go doing everything at once. Ya ain't God. Get yourself better first, then you will find your family." A certain confidence in Jesse's voice rang through that was beyond debate. Hunter needed to heal. He needed rest.

God and Country

"Where are we?" Hannah quietly whispered to Angie.

"I have no idea, Baby." Angie wrapped the little girl in her arms. The place seemed to be a massive cavern constructed into a system of roads, parking lots, and rooms. The soldiers had taken the four into a very large room hewn from limestone, then locked them in behind what appeared to be a very formidable looking wooden door. In the dim yellow lighting, Hank could see ventilation ducting overhead and three cafeteria-style tables. Near the table were two buckets. A smell of sweat, urine and feces hung in the air. In the opposite corner of the room stood four others, apparently in the same situation as they were.

Hank walked over, spanning most of the distance between the two groups. A tall, thin man was the first to speak, arresting Hank's short trek.

"Let me guess. Detainees?"

Hank nodded an affirmative.

"Don't hold your breath for a lawyer…and you might be waiting a while for any questioning."

The first part of the statement was a joke. There was no due process in a country ruled by tyranny. The only expectation from such a place was cruelty. On the other hand, no interrogation? That made no sense. As if to answer this question Hank had silently posed, the man continued.

"They simply don't have the officers to complete interrogations. Bachman has managed to snipe or assassinate so many of them, they need all of their officers for logistics and operations."

There was that name again. It seems the crazy rumors had been true. Aaron Bachman had been a Kansas City celebrity. For a decade, he had been a star left fielder known for his uncanny accuracy to throw home. Hank had actually met him once after managing to score VIP lounge tickets at Kannfield Stadium. He still remembered the only words Bachman had said to him as they shook hands: "It's damned hot in here." It seems that the All Star left fielder had managed to trade in his outfielders glove for a rifle.

"So what happens to us now?" Hank asked.

God and Country

"You stay here. We have been here two weeks. We are fed and watered like cattle once a day. If we are lucky, they empty the bucket...". Then the man paused, "What's your name?"

"Hank."

"I'm Jim. Hank, we need to come to an understanding."

Jim stood up and walked toward Hank, his wiry frame towering over Hank by almost a foot.

"When the food bag comes here tomorrow, we are going to get our share."

Hank immediately realized the challenge, a staking of claim. He responded by reaching out to shake the taller man's hand, making eye contact, all the while bearing down his grip firmly.

"And I imagine we will get our share as well."

Hank maintained the strength of his grip, smiling the entire time; his eyes probed into Jim's, until Jim showed discomfort.

Jim nodded in agreement, and Hank relented.

"Now that we have that out of the way, why don't you tell me what is going on, Jim?" Hank inquired amicably.

"Well, have you ever heard of the Subtropolis?"

Hank shook his head.

"Almost three square miles of underground warehousing and food storage. Some parts are almost 160 feet underground. Right next to Planet Fun amusement park."

Hank knew that location. Northeast of downtown off I-435.

Jim continued, "Some of the Kansas National Guard, the 1st Infantry Division out of Fort Riley, and DHS forces have been trying to establish control of Kansas City since October."

"Kansas National Guard? What about the Missouri National Guard?"

"Our boys said to hell with the federal government when Obama was assassinated, and that power-hungry bitch Clinton simply pushed Biden aside and took over. We hold south of the city, Overland Park, Olathe, Lee's Summit, and Raytown...barely. We have support from

Leonard Wood, but the 1st Infantry Division has Bradleys. Thank God for Bachman."

"Bachman?"

"Yeah, like I said, he is giving the DHS hell. We were heading down to meet him. We almost made it, when we were picked up. Caught me with a shotgun. I was lucky we weren't shot right where we stood."

Hank had learned long ago that it was better to listen than to speak, but he nodded at that last statement. He had been lucky, too.

—

The sleep that night had brought Hunter a night of unnatural dreams. Hunter had dreamed that he was in a race. He was nearing the finish line, but there was no one around him, no one behind him, as he was running around a building. He realized it was a stadium, and he ran inside and onto a baseball field. The stadium was packed and, as he entered, they stood in applause. He ran around the field and toward home plate. There, Jesse was standing. As Hunter arrived at home plate, Jesse embraced him and spoke. It wasn't Jesse's voice though, but a rich, deep voice. Hunter heard Jesse's words again:

"I can create good things out of next to nothin."

The crowd went wild. Suddenly, Hunter was running with a knife out of the stadium. The crowd was following him.

And then Hunter was awake, eyes wide open. He felt refreshed. He lifted himself up, unable to discern what was real. Had Jesse been a dream, too? Hunter looked at the place where the stove had been. It was gone, but the tin cup was still half full, sitting next to him. The canvas cover was still there, the poncho liner was still behind him, but Jesse was gone. Okay, that part was not a dream. Hunter placed his hand to his head. No bump. It was gone. He moved cautiously to rise. No dizziness. Then Hunter realized that even the nagging pain in his injured left arm was gone.

"I've been drugged," Hunter thought as he stood, but he did not feel so. He felt normal, well-rested. As Hunter stood up, he realized he had to find his family. His daughter and wife, yes, Angie was to be his wife, needed him. His brother needed him. He had to go find them, rescue them

God and Country

somehow. Hunter moved toward the door, then turned back. He picked up the poncho liner, the canvas cover, and, as an afterthought, the half-eaten cup of noodles.

Hunter opened the shed door to outside. There, in the dark, the hummer was still parked. Condensation covered the windshield. That indicated it was early morning. Predawn. Everything was there. Hunter made sure. Checking with the red lens flashlight, still in the floorboard of the hummer, everything appeared to be inside. Ammunition, weapons, everything except his family…and a single M4 rifle. If DHS had taken his family, why hadn't they discovered the vehicle; why hadn't they discovered Hunter? What had the old man told him? Had he dreamed about him, too?

Hunter stepped back from the passenger door of the hummer. This was too much. Perhaps his head had not healed after all. His dream was not fading into the drift of forgetful fog the way normal dreams do. It was still lucid, bright, more vivid than ever. Hunter got in the driver's seat of the hummer, warmed the diesel, then started the engine. He did not know where his family was, but Hunter knew he had to go to Kannfield Stadium.

"Uncle Hank, I'm hungry." Hannah offered not so much a complaint but a statement of fact. Yes, they were hungry. Their captors had brought food back at noon the next day, but there was pitifully little. Now Hank understood why Jim had been so direct about fair portions of food. Earlier that day, they worked out a remarkably equitable system of dividing food that Hank's mother had used with him and his brother as kids. One person divides the food, the other person selects the choice portion.

The memory of his mother brought Hank to tears. They had gone to be with her. Their stepdad had said if things ever got tough, they could come and be with them in Arkansas. He had been a Master Sergeant in the Army Reserve, and Hank knew damned well he would do his best to take care of her, but still, she was his mother. They had left Iowa in October. It was now February. What had happened since then?

God and Country

And, what about Hunter? How had Hunter not been discovered? It was as if the sergeant had no curiosity or desire to look any further for other people. Hank was quite sure he had seen the rear edge of their vehicle parked behind the shed from where he was. It made no sense. Was Hunter okay? Did he ever wake up?

—

Hunter had just left Sibley, Missouri. That is what the road sign had said. There were no vehicle tracks after the road became asphalt, so Hunter could not find any other reason to not go to Kannfield Stadium. Hunter was convinced that he had some brain damage still, dizzy or not. It did not matter. Call it a hunch. Some counselor once told him in high school to follow his dream so…fuck it. Hunter was following his dream.

Hunter verified he was traveling south by the predawn light on his left. About ten miles to I-70. Not that Hunter would take I-70. There were said to be DHS and UN patrols at most every exit. Hunter would parallel the interstate about a mile or two north and work his way toward Independence. He would need to cross the interstate to reach the stadium. The approaching dawn was making his blackout drive unnecessary, so he switched it off as he reached an intersection. Before proceeding through the intersection, he paused to think.

Hunter thought about what all had happened over the last four months. He had killed other people. He had lost his wife. No telling what Hannah was going through, losing her mother and not knowing if her dad was dead or alive. Why was all of this happening? And now. Tears filled Hunter's eyes. His entire family had been taken God knows where. Hunter, sure as hell, didn't have a clue.

Hunter put the vehicle in drive and turned east. He drove into the Independence city limits feeling like a fool. What in the hell was he doing? Nobody literally follows a dream. Yet this was different. There were no counselors, no religions. There was only Hunter, and he was helpless.

Hunter started to speak as he drove. "Ya know…." Hunter did not know if he was talking to himself or not, then a sudden realization came

God and Country

upon him. "Oh my God, am I praying?" he thought, and then decided "What the hell. I'm about out of options."

"Ya know," Hunter repeated aloud. "I could use some help right now. I don't know why the fu…" Hunter caught himself. "I mean, I don't know where to go, what to do. I need to find my family, my woman, my little girl." Hunter paused, "I need help." Then, looking up, Hunter hit the brakes. An overturned trailer and several vehicles, an impromptu barricade, had been set up in the middle of the road, and he had almost crashed into it.

Hunter's adrenaline was pumping so hard his side hurt. After gathering himself, he put the hummer in reverse, then, thinking for a moment, he put the vehicle into park and stepped out. Walking up to a vehicle with flattened tires, Hunter pushed himself atop the silver Monte Carlo's hood and stood atop the barricade. That was when Hunter noticed the advertisement on the food trailer. On the trailer's top side was a large painted picture of an old man. "Uncle Jesse's," the top banner proclaimed. Hunter took a knee, atop the vehicle, not quite comprehending what he had seen. Then he stood again.

The image of the familiar old man was still there, still smiling and staring at the sky. And the sign's banner remained the same: "Uncle Jesse's Chilis and Soups."

"No way," Hunter muttered, stepped back, stumbled, and fell onto the hood of the wrecked Monte Carlo.

Hank had been looking for a way to escape. The door would not budge. The limestone seemed impenetrable to any digging. The ventilation system seemed to be the only way. The ductwork had been hung from the ceiling, about ten feet high. It was two feet wide maximum, maybe 18 inches tall. Even if he could reach the ducting, the anchor straps would never hold his weight, and it was much too narrow for him. Maybe when he was six years old, he could have…Hannah?

No, even with Hannah on his shoulders and him pushing her up with his hands, they would not be tall enough. Hank looked around, then to Jim.

God and Country

Hunter got up, walked back to the hummer, and got inside.

"Okay, what do I do? What do I do?!" Hunter was terrified. His heart pounded. This was straight out of the Twilight Zone. No way this was an accident. He didn't believe in ghosts, or magic, or God, so he couldn't believe this. But, Hunter couldn't disbelieve it, either.

Hunter backed the vehicle up. A loud pop. The vehicle's smooth roll changed to a mushy movement. "Really?" It was obvious what had happened. He had punctured a tire.

Hunter got out. Sure enough, the rear driver's side tire had been punctured by something. What was that? A crossbow bolt? Hunter went back to the driver's side, grabbed his rifle, then took cover at the side of the vehicle, scanning for who had shot his tire.

Then Hunter realized something. Whoever shot his tire could have killed him, but didn't. A calm came over him.

"Perhaps all of this is just a dream anyway," Hunter thought to himself. "Been having some crazy ones lately."

Hunter propped the rifle against the side of the hummer. He took off his jacket, reached in, and put the poncho liner over him. Hunter took his knife, cut a hole in the middle of the piece of canvas, and put it over him too, wearing it like a poncho. He secured the knife and sheath in his belt and walked away from the vehicle, and toward Kannfield Stadium. If this was God, a dream, or simply a bad concussion, he would go with it. What other option did he have? Then, as an afterthought, Hunter turned back to the truck, reached in, and got the half-eaten cup of Ramen Noodles. In spite of everything, Hunter smiled as he thought to himself, "Uncle Jesse sure does make a mean soup."

Hunter had made his way through Independence, all the while feeling he was being watched. He kept moving forward at a determined pace, noting the I-70/I-435 sign ahead. "What if there were patrols ahead?" Hunter thought. There was no answer. Not yet. Hunter continued his walk onto the I-70 overpass without incident. He walked down the grass embankment to the unfenced parking lot of the stadium complex. The baseball stadium appeared to have been damaged by explosions and fire. Damaged, but still standing. It looked abandoned. Passing the checkpoint shack, he walked toward the gate entrance to the complex itself. Hunter felt that he was being watched yet again and raised his hands as he walked through the turnstile.

"Keep walking forward," a voice ordered, female, authoritative.

Hunter kept walking toward some tattered canopies, still managing to stand over the winter and apparent attack.

"I am looking for my family." Hunter continued to walk past the tattered canopies.

"We don't know you," the voice said.

"Maybe we should kill him now," another male voice added.

"Uncle Jesse told me to come here," Hunter offered.

With that came the sound of people whispering, murmuring.

The voice revealed herself. She was in her mid thirties, tall, fit, strikingly attractive. She wore a camouflage hunting jacket and BDU trousers. Her long black hair framed a seductively beautiful face that smudges of camouflage soot could not hide.

"Uncle Jesse?" the woman responded.

"I just spoke with him yesterday. He told me to come here." Hunter decided to not tell the woman that he had had a dream. He sounded crazy enough without sounding like Martin Luther King Jr.

Again, more murmuring.

"Follow me." They walked to a door and up a flight of stairs. Exiting on the second floor, she walked toward a distant concession area.

"Mind your step," the woman indicated a section of walkway that had been bombed.

Hunter skirted the danger and continued. Under a section of canopy, they walked past empty vending areas to the men's restroom.

"Safest place to be," Tracy commented.

Hunter wondered why he had been taken here. The woman walked over to the inside wall where the automatic sinks hung. Next to a wall mounted paper towel dispenser was something under a canvas cover very similar to the one Hunter was wearing. A body. A pair of familiar brown leather boots, worn and ripped, protruded from underneath.

"Uncle Jesse has been dead for two days." The woman removed the canvas. It was Jesse. The hair, face, hands. The olive drab army jacket. Hunter could only stare.

"So now, I want to know how you knew to find us. How you knew about Uncle Jesse?"

The woman had pulled her M9 Beretta from her side and pulled back the hammer. Hunter understood the slightest pressure could drop the single action trigger and end his life. "You said you saw him yesterday. You are a liar. Now tell us who you are."

"Why don't we just slow down with the drama, Tracy." A new voice echoed in the concreted room. In walked a confident man, solidly built, with a pleasant smile and piercing blue eyes. His rather thick beard could not disguise the person.

"I know you." Hunter couldn't help himself, forgetting his danger for a moment. "You're famous, man."

"Not so much anymore. I'm Aaron." The MLB All-Star offered his hand.

"Hunter Rich. I'm a fan."

"Now what is this about seeing dead people walking around?"

Hunter explained the story about meeting Jesse. He explained what had happened to his family. He perhaps talked too much, but it seemed that Aaron was listening to every word.

"Is there anything else?" Aaron asked.

Hunter hesitated. It was crazy. Then he stated: "I saw Jesse in a dream. That is how I knew to come here." Hunter told him about his dream of running into the baseball stadium.

Aaron paused, thinking. Then he spoke. "Right before Uncle Jesse died, he said something to me. He said 'I have to go and take care of someone. I will meet him at *home*.' I thought Jesse was talking about going to heaven."

God and Country

Later that evening, Hunter sat and listened while Aaron talked. "Everyone thinks that I am some kind of hero," the MLB star explained. "The truth is, I am an average shot at best. I am here for marketing purposes. Tracy here is the real death angel. 2014 NCAA Rifle Champion Marksman. And she has not lost her touch. She has 43 official kills and has demoralized the entire DHS occupation.

"Don't sell yourself short, Wonder Boy." Tracy piped in, touching the baseball player's face with one finger, which managed to leave the ball player with a smile. Turning to Hunter, she smiled and said "You ought to see Aaron throw a grenade. A regular M203."

"I am here for my family: my woman, my daughter, my brother. They have been taken."

"Military gets taken to Leavenworth. We think civilians get taken somewhere along here." Aaron pointed to the map northeast of downtown Kansas City.

"You think?" Hunter said, as if he had been distracted in thought.

"Not exactly sure where."

Hunter felt something, like a hunch. He had no idea where his family was, but he knew he had to go. He didn't know where, but he knew he had to leave immediately.

"I know this is crazy, but I think I can find where they are," Hunter explained.

"Absolutely nothing sounds crazy to me now," Aaron confessed.

"Then, I need you to trust me. And I… need to leave now."

"Ummm, okay."

Hunter shook Aaron's hand and blurted, "My mom is going to freak out when I tell her I met you." Then Hunter turned and walked away.

Aaron turned to Tracy. "Any idea where he is going?"

Tracy shook her head.

"Follow him, and take this," Aaron said, handing Tracy a small black box with a blinking red LED. "We will know where you are."

God and Country

Hannah stood atop Jim's shoulders, while Hank supported Jim. In her hand she had a pair of extra long trousers. Jim's trousers. Hannah was trying to throw one leg of the trousers over the ductwork. It was quite a questionable spectacle.

"I can't do it, Uncle Hank. I just can't throw that good."

"Haul her down a minute," Hank said. "Catalina, can you give me one of your sneakers?"

Hank unlaced the sneaker, then tied the lace to one eyelet. The other end of the lace, he tied to a pant leg.

"Back up." The little girl climbed up Jim's lanky body, onto his shoulders. Jim steadied her with his hands.

"One, two, three…"

"I'm sorry, Uncle Hank."

"That's okay, Hannah. Let's do it again."

This time when Hannah threw the shoe, it went over the ductwork.

"Lift the pant's up now, Hannah….Good! Now, can you grab the shoe?"

The little girl grabbed the shoe, pulling the pant leg over and down the other side.

Hank looked up at Jim, whom he was supporting. "You do understand that my pants would never have been long enough, right?" Hank asked.

"As long as I get them back," Jim replied, straddled atop Hank in his boxers.

Hank let out a quiet laugh.

Hannah climbed down, and the men repositioned.

"Now, you are not as light as the little girl, so let's get this right the first time," Jim stated.

—

Hunter was walking. In his pocket he carried a GPS tracker. Hunter knew he needed to travel north, that was it. He walked down a road in the dark. In the distance, a dog barked. There were few dogs nowadays. It had been a rough winter. Up ahead, there was a group of men gathered around a trash can fire. Hunter was only armed with his knife. Should he avoid them? No. Just keep walking.

Hunter continued walking toward the group. There were five of them. Two had shotguns. Hunter was no more than thirty feet from them. One man, a tough-looking Mexican, seemed to look straight at him. Hunter continued his pace. He was directly across the street from them. He could see the tattoo of an ornate cross on one man's neck from the glare of the fire. The Mexican man took a step forward, glaring at him. Then suddenly, the man appeared uncomfortable as to what he saw. He shifted his gaze slightly, focusing away from Hunter. It was impossible. The man couldn't see him.

"Jesus," Hunter muttered to himself, unsure if he was blaspheming or praying.

Hank had managed to pull down the ductwork, and Hannah was inside, climbing upward at an angle. It was dark, and Hannah had to find a way out of there on her own. Uncle Hank said that meant she would have to kick open a grate or something and jump down. The duct leveled out, and she moved forward, leaving the last bit of light from the room she had left. Suddenly, Hannah's hand moved forward to feel nothing. A drop-off. She was terrified. There was no room to turn around. If she went down that, she would have to go head first. Could she hang on to the walls and crawl like a spider upside down? Hannah remembered all the times her dad and Uncle Hank had done scary things. They had been afraid as well. It was Hannah's time to do things that made her afraid.

Hannah lowered her upper body down through the ductwork. Pressing her hands against the walls, she could keep herself from falling. Hopefully. She let hold of one of her feet still gripping above. Then the other. Uncle Hank had taken her shoes and her socked feet had no grip. Hannah spread out her knees and legs as far as she could to get a grip against the metal walls and began walking down the ductwork. How far down. She did not know. Looking down, she saw a faint yellow light… then she fell.

Hunter approached what looked like a six-foot chain link fence. It had three sections of barbed wire facing both ways. Hunter stopped for a moment as if thinking, or was he listening? He took off his canvas tarp, approached a metal support pole, and threw the canvas over the barbed strands on either side of the pole, climbing over. He moved forward. It was dark, but there was something posted on a billboard ahead. He moved closer. Did that say "Planet Fun?" He had been here before.

Hunter waited quietly. He was listening for a small voice inside his head or something. Instead, Hunter realized he had to urinate. Normally, Hunter would just take a piss wherever. He was alone, right? Something however, felt wrong about taking a leak in the middle of an amusement park. He instinctively looked for a bathroom sign. That's when Hunter saw the light.

Not "*The Light*," but a faint yellow glow coming from under the door of what appeared to be a small storage building. As Hunter came closer, he noticed that there was a hum coming from the building as well. Lights normally meant people, so Hunter carefully approached the door. He pulled his knife and slowly reached for the door. Suddenly, the door opened on its own. The soldier exiting the doorway did not see Hunter immediately, but as soon as he did, he attempted to unsling his rifle. Hunter, knife at ready, pushed forward with the blade into the man's neck. The soldier reached toward Hunter's arm with one hand, his other hand moving to his bloody punctured throat. Hunter made a strong, short backstroke with his blade, then in again. Hunter eased the dying body to the floor.

Hannah felt her head. It was wet. It hurt. She moved her arms to push herself up. A light was ahead. She crawled forward inside the level ductwork and approached a metal vent cover. She looked through it. It was a small room with a desk underneath her. She could do this. She moved forward, positioned her legs against the grill, and kicked. Instantly, the grill popped free. Now she just needed to squeeze through. Legs first, hang on, use her arms. There, now drop.

Hannah was standing atop the desk wondering where she was. She hadn't traveled very far, had she? Hannah looked up at the ductwork. It moved straight up. Hannah opened the office door. The room door should have been right next to here, but it wasn't. Hannah looked back in the office. How far had she fallen?

Hannah recognized that she was still in the cave. It still had rock walls. Did caves have more than one story? Maybe like a two-story house but underground? Maybe there would be a staircase somewhere where she could climb back up. She just had to make sure she didn't get lost.

What was this? Hunter had entered the room and looked around. It appeared to be a ventilator system: a huge filter, fan, and ductwork. But for what? It looked to be going straight down. This was it. Going down. The power switch for the fan unit was clearly marked on the side. After powering down, Hunter managed to unscrew four metal screws securing a portion of the sheet metal box. Hunter peered inside. Pitch black down there. Straight down. How would he manage to…

At the side of the wall was a coiled firehose. Hunter dropped it down, leaving it connected to the spigot. At what he thought was thirty feet, he thought he heard the thunk of the nozzle hitting something.

Hunter climbed down the ductwork. Whatever this place was, it had to be massive to need so much ventilation. Reaching the bottom, more humming and a soft glow of yellowish light. Moving forward, Hunter suddenly began sliding again. Ahead, a second fan. Hunter pushed his hands against the bottom of the ductwork to slow his slide. He came to rest inches from a rapidly operating fan blade as tall as he was. What now? His poncho liner. No, this time it would need to be the liner and the canvas. Hunter threw the canvas into the spinning blades. This made the blades slow down enough for Hunter to throw the poncho liner into the moving motor belt. The fan blades moved slower and slower to where Hunter

God and Country

could stop them with his hand. Hunter climbed through the blades, kicking the large screen out.

He was in a cavern of sorts, but also a parking lot. Hunter looked down the long corridor. There was someone walking down the corridor toward him. A child. No. It couldn't be! It was Hannah.

"Daddy!" Hannah was running as fast as she could. "Oh, Daddy, I knew you would find me."

"My sweet Baby Girl." Tears streamed down his face. "Daddy loves you so much." As they embraced, Hunter realized something. Not only was he happy to be holding his little girl again, he was extremely grateful.

Even in the pale yellow light, Hunter could see his daughter's bloody, matted hair. He gently pushed her hair out of the way to examine a deep gash in her scalp line. It needed stitches, but they didn't have time for that now. "Hannah, where are Uncle Hank, Angie, and Catalina?"

"I fell down the vent back that way, Daddy. I guess up there somewhere?"

"Let's go back to where you fell, okay baby?"

As they were walking down the corridor, they heard voices. Hunter and Hannah took cover behind a parked semi truck. Hunter could hear the footsteps coming closer. "It came from over here, I think," one of the voices announced. "You two, check the ventilation room. You...check out level 4. The rest...on me." Hunter could see the sets of boots directly in front of him moving off toward where he had been. Another group left the opposite direction. Level 4 maybe? The sound of the hurried shuffling faded to echoes and another, more methodic sound of footsteps. They were searching this parking level. Hunter positioned himself and Hannah between the set of tires by the fifth wheel. "Jesus," Hunter thought to himself. There was no way they would not be seen. Hunter moved his bloody hand subconsciously to the knife tucked away in his belt. Footsteps moved closer. Hunter could see a pair of boots stopping at the back of the trailer and instinctively pulled Hannah a bit closer. He had to fight. "Not too bright, bringing a knife to a gun fight." Hunter managed a tight grin at the movie quote that had come to his mind. The pair of boots was alertly positioned back from the trailer. Hunter realized that taking the soldier by surprise was not going to happen. Still...Hunter braced himself to spring. Closer, ready and....

Gunshots. The menacing pair of boots turned around and quickly moved to the center of the parking level. It was difficult to determine where the shots had come from. A burst of automatic fire, then a huge concussive explosion that made Hunter's ears ring. The soldiers searching the parking area ran toward Level 2, which was where Hunter suspected he needed to go.

Hunter and Hannah stepped out cautiously. The enormous cavern system began to fill with a deafening, murderous cacophony. There was shouting, gunshots. Hunter felt the need to hurry, so he and Hannah trotted along. Running around a corner, Hunter and Hannah nearly ran into a half dozen uniformed DHS agents, who simply ran by them as if they were not there. Except one agent. The agent stopped his double-time up the graded incline and turned to Hunter. The agent simply looked at his arm incredulously as it slowly stretched out and pointed. Then his arm suddenly dropped to his side. Hunter looked in the direction the agent had indicated. About a hundred feet away was a door marked "Exit." The uniformed agent, terrified, turned and took off in a dead run up the ramp.

Hunter and Hannah walked to the exit door and up a flight of stairs. The relative silence brought a relief from the murderous scream of battle. "Level 2?" No, didn't seem right. Hunter couldn't explain. "Level 1?" The stairs continued on, but Hunter and Hannah did not. Opening the door unmuted the explosions once more. Hunter turned left, the way he had entered the stairwell two levels below. He ran down the incline, turned right, and ran down the corridor through the blistering noise of battle. A door on the left, double bolted. Hunter paused, ran to the door, and unbolted it. He opened the door. A smell of urine and foul odor assaulted his olfactories as his eyes adjusted to the low yellow light. Dimly, Hunter was able to see people huddled against the far wall. He walked over and touched one on the shoulder. The person got up. He touched another.

Over twenty people. Not his family. The people followed Hunter out into the noise.

Hunter unlatched a second room, and again, not his family. Feeling a building anxiety, Hunter walked down the cavernous passage. About fifty people stayed behind Hunter, following him. At the end of the hall was a final door. Hunter opened it. Hank was there, wielding a table leg over his head. He dropped the makeshift weapon and smiled. The two brothers embraced. Catalina, and Angie walked forward.

Hunter walked over to Angie and kissed her tenderly. He held Angie in his arms and said, "Don't leave me like that, damnit." Hannah was hugging both of their legs. This was indeed who Hunter had been searching for...his family.

The family walked out with others following behind. The shooting was over for the most part. An occasional pop was heard from a lower level. Coming up from below was a large group of DHS agents and soldiers, hands on their heads, being escorted around the corner by militia. Each of the militia wore a wide cloth tied to their left arm. Royal blue. Hunter walked toward the upper level, what he hoped was the exit. The place seemed set up like an oversized parking garage with side "caverns?" Hunter's ear's still rang as they walked up the final ramp and down toward the concreted exit. Someone was standing in front of the exit. It was difficult to make out who the person was because of the bright lights which shone behind him. As they walked up to the man, Hunter recognized the dirty white Kings baseball jersey: #5. Aaron Bachman had a huge shit-eating grin on his face. He offered a handshake. They walked out together to a spontaneous eruption of cheering and gunfire.

"Tracy and a platoon of her militia followed behind you," Aaron explained.

―

It was about 9 a.m when the family had made it back to Kannfield Stadium. They were in a conference room.

"We wasted some time taking out those thugs out on Whitmire Drive," Tracy stated, having entered the room. She walked up to Hunter

God and Country

and Aaron and continued to speak. "Had to take them out quietly." She touched a finger to her tongue and then ran the finger slowly along the string of her crossbow. Hunter recognized the crossbow bolt as similar to what had taken out his tire. Then Hunter's mind recalled everything that had happened since then, and he felt lightheaded. Angie, who had instinctively come up beside her man, held onto Hunter.

"Whoa, guy!" Aaron remarked. "Looks like you guys could use a little shut eye. The umm….The…" Aaron almost used the word "refugees." "The people we rescued are by the east turnstile area. We got your family in the Mark White Lounge. Tracy will show you the way."

Tracy walked the family to the large room that overlooked the baseball field. Inside the center of the room were some of their belongings and weapons from their vehicle. Hunter looked at Tracy.

"What? You didn't think we were going to leave your hummer back in Independence, did you?" Tracy stated with a seductive smile. "We have it parked on the east side with the refugees."

Chapter 12

Wandering

The family helped themselves to some MREs and water from a brown, five gallon military water can. Afterwards, Hank and Catalina found one corner of the room, while Hunter propped himself in the other corner, holding Angie and Hannah, who was still nursing a pack of dehydrated strawberries as if they were a popsicle.

Sleep came to Hunter easily, but the dreams did not escape him. He dreamed of the farm house on the hill. It was Christmas time. All the worker's families were there. Martha was reading the Christmas story. Hunter looked up to see Angie holding Hannah at the doorway. They were smiling. The reading continued: *"Rise, take the child and his mother, and flee into Egypt, and remain there until I tell you, for Herod is about to search for the child, to destroy him."* Martha's voice blended in with another voice, a familiar one. His mother's. Then Hunter was in a field. His mother appeared walking toward him, with her husband Jason, who was in his Army uniform. His mother looked at him, smiling. Behind them in the distance, an explosion. His mom's expression changed to one of fear. Her voice carried an unfamiliar tone, urgency. "Flee, Hunter!"

Hunter woke up immediately. It was bright inside the lounge. There were no coverings over the expansive windows overlooking the ballpark. The family was already up. He had slept in.

"Hey, guy," Hank said cheerfully through a mirror, shaving his head with a dedicated straight razor.

Hunter looked at Hank. "We need to go. Now."

"Huh?" Hank put his razor on the table, turned around, and grabbed a towel, polishing his work. "Why?"

"I don't know why. All I know is we need to leave."

"Leave to where, Hunter? I mean, this is a good place. People like us here. I mean, we are in the Mark White Lounge, for God sakes. Considering things, we seem to have it good."

"You know how I found you guys? How no one knew where to look?" Hunter was packing a large duffle bag with blankets and MREs.

"I didn't quite understand what you were trying to tell me at the time."

"Neither did I," Hunter interjected while he continued to pack. "No one could find you, but I did. I just knew. And I know now."

"You just wake up and say all this. You are crazy, Hunter. What? Do you just dream up this stuff?"

Hunter paused, wondered what else he should share, then responded "Basically, yeah."

Hank put his arm on his brother and turned to the family. "I guess we need to leave."

The family gathered up the weapons and food, using the blankets to wrap and sack materials. Hank lugged the five-gallon water can behind the others, as Hunter led the way down the spiral walkway out to the east side of the stadium.

At ground level, hundreds of men, women, and children were camped under the base level of the stadium. People were beginning to notice Hunter coming down the walkway, and they started to get up.

"Are you leaving?" asked the tall, thin man that Hank seemed to know.

"Yes."

"Why?"

More people began to gather around the family now.

"Where are you going?"

People began to mutter. A familiar face pushed its way through the crowd.

"Hey, man," Aaron greeted Hunter. "What's up?"

"We are leaving to find our family in Arkansas."

God and Country

"Seems a bit sudden," Bachman responded as Tracy moved beside him. "Did you have another dream?"

Hunter was silent.

"Yeah, I thought so. I would say you were crazy, but not after what all I saw. Hell, I would go with you, but I can't leave KC. The people need me here." Aaron shook hands with the brothers, while Tracy smiled and nodded at Hunter.

Aaron walked the family through the turnstile area, past the concrete barricades, and out to the east parking lot to their vehicle. As the family packed their vehicle, they noticed that most of the people they had rescued had gathered up the food and blankets they had been given. The group gathered next to the family's hummer.

Finishing their packing, the family took their seats inside the vehicle. As Hank moved to the driver's side door, he addressed the tall man who had helped Hannah escape. "Jim, where does everyone think they are going?"

"Hell, Hank, they haven't got a clue, but if you ask me, I would say they want to go somewhere with you guys. It seems your brother has become quite the hero."

"We can't take you with us. You will slow us down."

"I get it. Can't blame us for trying, though, right?"

Suddenly, overhead there was a tremendous sonic boom, followed by another. Then, two huge explosions hit the stadium.

"What the fuck was that?" Hank exclaimed, the heat from the explosions some 200 yards away created an uncomfortable warmth as he turned to face an explosion of dust and debris. Hank turned to see the east side of the stadium completely collapsed. Black smoke and fire poured from the rubble, and a cloud of gray dust moved out over the crowd in the parking lot. Hank took a moment to collect himself, to reconcile himself with the present reality. Thirty minutes ago the family had been having breakfast, oblivious to what was about to happen. Except Hunter. He had known.

God and Country

Hank turned to Hunter, standing opposite the vehicle from him. "How?"

"I don't know." Hunter looked just as bewildered as his brother. "But, we have to help."

The family and refugees spent the next two days working with Aaron to find those who had been killed or injured by the explosions. Casualties included seventeen dead, fourteen wounded, and six missing. Of the dead, most had been killed in the explosion or crushed in the collapse. Several fighters had limbs crushed under collapsing concrete. Five field amputations had to be performed to free individuals. Two of those would not survive the day. Another five people had been bathing in the first floor restroom area, which had not collapsed. They were concussive, bleeding from the ears and nose, but would survive.

Five of the burn victims had been in such horrible pain that Aaron had euthanized them. He had come back with tears in his eyes.

"I am so sorry," Hunter said.

"Sorry?" Aaron looked surprised and managed a painful laugh. "If it weren't for you, over three hundred people would be dead here."

Hunter didn't know what to say, so he didn't.

—

Two days later, the family's hummer drove at a snail's pace, followed by a crowd of about three hundred people. Angie drove the hummer, which carried the most elderly and afflicted. Hank and Catalina walked with Jim and his family, with whom they had been imprisoned. Hunter and Hannah walked alongside the hummer, keeping pace. They talked.

"Where are we going, Daddy?" Hannah asked her dad.

Hunter had always felt a strong bond with his daughter, but after what all had happened, Hunter felt such a wave of overwhelming emotion that tears came to his eyes.

"Belton. Right up this road a ways."

Angie commented over her shoulder out the window.

"Did you dream that, babe?"

God and Country

"No," Hunter replied uncertainly. "Just a stop on our way to mom's."

Angie pressed. "You know, we are leading three hundred, hungry people to this place. It is past noon, and some of these people are starving."

Hunter looked at the passenger door behind Angie. They had managed to fit eleven people in the hummer seating area and cargo compartment. Four more rode the tailgate. The people in the vehicle listened to the conversation as Hunter and Angie talked, knowing their future was being discussed. Because of that, some things were left unsaid. Most of the supplies at the stadium had been lost in the attack. Aaron simply couldn't feed the group. This "caravan" of people had wanted to go with the family. It seemed that was what was "supposed" to happen.

"Angie, I don't know what to do about that." Which was the honest truth. Hunter was afraid. He felt like a kid lost in the woods with nothing left to hold onto but a security blanket, knowing he would feel lost without it. Then Hunter spoke again.

"But I don't think we have any choice."

Angie did not respond, but her look said it all. They did have a choice. Their family could get into the vehicle and speed away. They could find Hunter's mom. They could….Angie looked at the aged passengers in the vehicle, the children on the tailgate. No, they couldn't leave these people behind. She herself had been rescued.

Angie spoke up. "No, we really don't have a choice, do we?" she sighed.

—-

The day plodded along as the weary caravan moved forward. Hank came forward as well as Tracy.

"Hey," Hank said concisely.

Hunter looked at Tracy. "You came with us?"

"I couldn't leave you possibly stranded. After all, I put a nice-sized hole in your rear tire."

Hunter gave a smirk, but Angie looked pissed off, eyes straight ahead, slowly rolling the vehicle forward.

"We have about thirty people armed," Hank interrupted the awkward silence. "About 6 M4s, a dozen or so ARs, otherwise, hunting rifles, pistols, and shotguns."

"Not exactly an army," Hunter replied.

"No, and I don't know how we are going to feed them. We already gave them the few MRE's in the truck."

"I know. We can make Belton and see what happens."

"Yeah, I caught that," Hank interrupted. "And, I don't understand it. You have the lead, brother. But, we ain't gonna make it there today at any rate. Maybe tomorrow. And the people need to rest along the way."

"I know," Hunter replied.

Hank held in his frustration. "Okay, but we need to rest tonight."

Hunter looked at his watch, a cheap military-style timepiece, no doubt made in China. The watch had held up well. It's glowing illuminated the time: 9:17 p.m. on an unusually warm evening in mid-February. Tomorrow was Valentine's day. The overcast sky gave a mugginess to the 60 degree temperature, and it played on and off threatening rain. The caravan had moved through it all along Interstate 49 at a slow, steady plod that day and into the evening. Weariness had set upon the travelers bone-deep. For many of the travelers, it had been a marathon of ill-treatment, violence, and malnutrition for several weeks. The hummer had gained more passengers on its hood and hard top cover. The large group looked very similar to the starving caravans of third-world countries that were attempting escape to freedom. Indeed, that was exactly what they were. The caravan approached an overpass that crossed their path just as the sprinkling grew more into a gentle steady rain.

"Where are we now?" Hunter asked his brother walking alongside him.

"Near Grandview. A rest stop?" Hank asked.

Hunter nodded. The vehicle pulled to the far side of the overpass in an attempt to hide the vehicle from unwanted notice. That would do little good against anyone passing by considering there were about 150 people under each side of the overpass. A guard rotation was set up. At least the caravan could dry out for the night. Hunter slept in the vehicle with his family. Hank took Hunter's watch to start the guard rotation, a rotation that Hunter would participate in at 4:00 a.m. He dozed, holding Angie. Hannah was a lump of sleep next to them...Hunter was thankful.

The morning was a peaceful, lazy morning. Which was a problem. The caravan was exhausted. People wanted to sleep. Both Hank and Hunter knew they had to move. It was a slow, painful "stand-to." Angie and Catalina fit as many people into the hummer as possible. Tracy came to help, but the look Angie gave her communicated her help was not needed.

"I would keep my eye on that bitch. She has the hots for your man," Catalina remarked.

"If she so much as tries anything, I will shove one of those arrows she has in her eye socket and clean out the other side."

Catalina winced. "Damn, girl."

Angie straightened herself a bit, as if to become more proper. "Let's just say I've had some time to think about it." She got in the driver's seat, started up the vehicle, and rolled it up the grass embankment to the highway. Catalina kept pace near the driver's side window. Once on the highway, Catalina continued their conversation.

"You know Hunter loves you more than anything. You can see that by the way he looks at you. I just wish..."

"What?"

"I wish Hank looked at me like that."

"Hank is just different. He seems like a person who is quiet and careful with his feelings. Once he makes up his mind, however, watch out."

"I am beginning to realize that. I just know if that Tracy bitch ever trics something with him, I will cut her ass dead."

"Amen, sister."

God and Country

The passengers in the vehicle listened to the conversation but kept their mouths shut.

The morning was slower than the day before. Mile markers were an eternity away, and by now the only thing filling the bellies of the travelers was a gnawing hunger. There was a light drizzle that hovered over the dreary day, drenching the weary pilgrims drops at a time.

"So, what about you, Hank. What is up with Catalina?"

Hank knew what his brother was asking, but needed the time to collect himself.

"What do you mean? We are together if that is what you mean."

"I know you two are sleeping together. I mean, are you serious about her?"

"I guess so. Don't know." Changing the subject, Hank offered, "I do know you better watch out, brother. Tracy wants your ass, and it is pissing Angie off. Did you see how Angie looked at her this morning?"

Hunter was distracted. On the other side of the road, Tracy had slowed down her pace to match Hunter's. She looked at him, a slight smile on her face. Hunter turned away, looking a bit uncomfortable. The brothers lowered their voices but continued talking.

"So, do you have any idea why Tracy left Aaron?" Hunter asked.

"I don't know that part, but she seems to be after you now."

"Yeah, I've noticed."

"Just be careful. It might be just something innocent, but it seems like something more to it."

Hunter thought about this for a while, then his mind wandered to what had happened in the last few days. It was as if he could only skim over the events, and not dwell on them for too long, being so far beyond explanation or comprehension.

And so the morning passed. The gnawing hunger played itself like a physical pain in the bellies of the caravan. Hunter could only imagine how the others felt, weakened from their long period of captivity. As he walked, his eyes searched for the Belton exit. There was a fireworks store supposably? Perhaps there, in the distance?

"Hi." A warm voice interrupted him.

"Umm, hi." Hunter said awkwardly, answering back to Tracy, avoiding eye contact.

"Are we gonna get there soon? I am so hungry," Tracy purred.

"That could be it up ahead."

"Ya know, what I could use is a nice warm bath and a massage."

"Look, Tracy. I am taken. My woman, umm…my wife, is right up there."

"Oh, I know, Hunter. I just don't care. I can keep a secret. Can you?"

"No, I won't."

"Tell who you gotta tell. I can be very useful to you on so many levels." Her eyes sparkled like diamonds as she turned her luscious mouth into a seductive smile. A finger went to her mouth. Tracy paused for a minute as Hunter walked away.

Tracy ended her seductive routine and talked plainly as Hunter walked ahead. "There is something about you, something you have. I saw it when you came to the stadium. How you knew Uncle Jesse? Then the way you just led us to where the prisoners were. Those five men around that fire should have killed you. You walked right past them as if they were not there. Hell, even when you left the stadium right before the attack."

"Weren't you with Bachman?" Hunter countered.

"That's over," Tracy stated dryly, without emotion. "Aaron was a good man. The people knew him. That gave him a certain power….but it's nothing like what you have. Let me be with you. We could do anything together. You could be a king, and I…"

"Again, I have a family."

"I can wait…wait until you want me."

Hunter hurriedly made his way toward the front of the caravan. In the distance was the billboard: "Firecracker City Fireworks." A somewhat redundant name, Hunter thought, trying to distract himself from the recent uncomfortable conversation.

God and Country

Hunter made his way up to the hummer. Angie had seen the entire episode with Hunter and Tracy.

"I want you to stay away from that bitch," Angie responded when Hunter walked up. Her eyes were smoldering with rage.

"I don't need to be told, babe, I love you, remember?"

"I'm not worried about you. It's her."

—

The last mile passed very slowly. Hunter stayed with the hummer, keeping pace. The refugees plodded their way forward, on their last legs. Walking up the exit ramp, Hunter took note of the surroundings. There was a truck stop next to the fireworks store, both appearing abandoned. A motel across the street stood, almost as abandoned, except for an older model Chevy truck. The truck's original color might have been blue, but the dirt and chipped paint had faded the color's absolute nature to more of a gray tone. Angie pulled the hummer to the far side of the parking lot. Hunter walked toward the truck and the motel office beyond. As he got closer, Hunter could make out a bumper sticker under a film of whitish dust. "Don't Blame Me. I Didn't Vote for Socialism." Hunter smiled and pulled open the door.

The outside sunlight filtered through the window, highlighting dust stirred up from the open door. Behind the counter, sat a man sporting a snap-backed green John Deere hat. His glasses were pushed down his nose a bit. His long sleeve shirt was definitely a seventies throwback, complete with pearl snap buttons. His eyes were curious, searching Hunter as he entered, yet with a broad, gentle smile that matched the wrinkles of his face and eyes.

"Can I help you?" the older man asked.

"I sure hope so. We are looking for a place to stay the night."

"That is why I stopped here myself. The name is Leroy, Leroy Bowers." The man smiled and offered his hand.

—

The people had settled outside the motel on the grass at the edge of the parking lot. Angie searched through the crowd to find Tracy. She had a

God and Country

few words to say to her. Yet Tracy wasn't in the crowd. Angie suddenly caught sight of someone walking around the far side of the motel. She walked across the parking lot and around the corner of the building. No one. Angie went around to the other side of the building. There were an identical number of hotel room doors as the front side had, but no one in sight. Angie turned her eye to the nearby wooded area.

—

As the men searched the place for keys, a conversation ensued. "So, how does a person have come to have this many people following them?"

The man listened as Hunter talked. And when Hunter finished, the man paused, what seemed quite a while. Then he smiled.

"Uncle Jesse? As in that 70's T.V. show with the confederate car? That Uncle Jesse?" Leroy asked in a heavy southern drawl, smiling broadly.

It had not once dawned on Hunter that the man he had met had somewhat resembled the late 70's television character. "Yeah, the guy owned a food truck in Kansas City," Hunter said dully, immediately feeling foolish.

Leroy chuckled. "Haven't seen that show in years."

"I'm not making this stuff up…"

"Now hold on, hold on. I didn't say I didn't believe you. Just funnin' you is all. Now, what do you think is causing all of this to happen?"

"I'm going crazy?"

"Probably."

"I mean, God is not real, right?"

"I never said I didn't believe in God. From my experience though, most people don't go looking for God unless they realize they need Him."

Leroy looked at Hunter and grinned. "You know, I bet you thought I was supposed to tell what you should do."

"Well, uhh, are you?"

God and Country

Leroy laughed. "I ain't got the foggiest notion of what you are supposed to do. I might recommend getting your people some food and these keys." Leroy had found the keys hidden in the bottom of a cabinet.

"Okay," Hunter replied

"I hope y'all like rice."

Angie walked into the wood line about fifty feet when she saw Tracy relieving herself.

Tracy looked up at Angie. "Jesus, girl. Can't a woman get some fucking privacy?" She took time to completely relieve herself, unworried about her visitor, who continued to stare at her.

"Are you wondering what a real woman looks like?" Tracy said contemptuously, pulling her jeans up. "Maybe I could make you useful after I am finished fucking your man."

"You fucking whore! You will stay away from him, I swear, I will fucking kill you."

"Oh, we can't have that, can we?" Tracy calmly smiled as Angie approached her. Tracy avoided Angie's oncoming fist, grabbing Angie's hair as the blonde attacker followed through, pulling Angie to the ground. Tracy waited for her attacker to get up, motioning her to come at her again.

"Is that all you got? Seriously?"

Again Angie ran at her. This time Tracy kicked her square in the chest, knocking Angie on her back and taking her breath away. Tracy took two steps over to her fallen attacker, firmly in control. "I can do this all day," Tracy said nonchalantly. "I just don't know if I have the time." Tracy kicked her in the ribs, then pushed Angie with her foot.

"You know, I was taking it easy on you. I could have broken three ribs with that last kick. Hell, I could have killed you at the very first."

"Well, why don't you then!" Angie hissed through tears of pain and frustration.

"I'm having fun," Tracy hesitated, "But I guess I could kill you now." Tracy pulled a rather dangerous looking combat knife from her belt and slowly knelt on both of Angie's shoulders. Tracy had a look of ecstasy

God and Country

as she put the knife's tip to Angie's throat. "And after I kill you, I will be with your man," Tracy said absently. "Later on, that little brat of yours will have an accident. Then he will be mine completely." Tracy smiled a cold smile, brought the blade to Angie's left eye, and pushed her body forward closer to Angie's face.

Tears began to form in Angie's eyes as she felt the cold terror of her fate.

"So, I will ask you again. Shall I kill you now?"

Angie slowly shook her head.

"I couldn't hear you, my little whore." Tracy shifted her knees again, pushing her crotch against Angie's chin.

Angie's frustration, pain, and humiliation brought more tears to her eyes. "No," Angie whispered.

"Say 'Please,' my little whore."

"No. Please," Angie begged in a whisper.

Tracy knew she had won. She brought up her other hand to Angie's face, gently wiped her tears, then caressed her wet finger against Angie's lower lip.

"Maybe I won't kill you," Tracy offered, shifting her body slightly forward yet a bit more. "Maybe..." Tracy's finger moved across Angie's lips. "I mean, you are pretty, in a homely sort of way."

Angie's eyes looked off, as if in thought, then slowly returned to Tracy's gaze. Angie opened her mouth a bit, her wet tongue slightly touching Tracy's finger, her eyes yearning to please.

Tracy's smile warmed over her cold eyes. "Aww, my cute little whore. If I could train you to play nice, you could..."

Then came a sick thud.

"Fuck playing nice, you sick bitch!" An angry voice yelled from behind.

Tracy's eyes crossed and turned partially up in her head, as blood began to trickle from her right ear. Tracy dropped the knife, which slightly nicked the top of Angie's cheek as it fell to the ground. Then, Tracy's body went limp, still straddling Angie's neck.

God and Country

Behind stood Catalina still grasping a three-foot piece of galvanized metal pipe with both hands. A groan came from Tracy as Catalina kicked her body to the side. Catalina, trembling, managed a shaky smile, still holding her weapon. "Hi Sis," Catalina managed.

Angie tried to push herself up from the ground, but didn't succeed. She lay there, propped up on one arm, tremors running throughout her body. Catalina knelt down with her for a long while, comforting her sister-in-law. Her trembling eased; her tears subsided. The sisters slowly managed to get up, and started to walk away.

After about a dozen steps, a groan came from behind them. The two sisters looked at each other. Catalina stopped and began to turn around, but Angie placed her hand on Catalina's shoulder, stopping her. Angie looked at Catalina, then Catalina slowly nodded. Angie gently took the pipe from Catalina's fingers, turned and walked back. Catalina paused, then followed her. After all, sisters had to stick together, no matter what.

The truck stop across the street had been ransacked, not yielding a single scrap of food. There were, however, some remaining stainless steel pots and containers that had once belonged to the adjacent "Steel Skillet" restaurant. Naturally, cooking the rice meant fuel, and in an environment where there was no electric nor gasoline, the options for fuel were limited. Wood was the choice. Of the 300 people there, Hank, Catalina, and Angie were among the first to volunteer for wood duty. They and six other people walked the edge of the woods looking for fuel. The family broke from the rest of the group.

"You what?!"

"She is dead. She had a knife to my throat and was going to rape and kill me."

Catalina interrupted, "She was one sick bitch."

"You killed her?" Hank asked Catalina.

"Actually, we both did," Angie said.

"You *both* killed her!? What did you do, take turns?"

God and Country

"Yes, we took turns. You godda problem with dat?" Catalina's voice rose defensively.

"So, what do we do?" Angie pleaded.

"Will they find the body?"

"We drug her back a bit more, but yeah. She, umm, it is directly in front of us about a hundred feet." Angie felt hopeless.

"Okay. At least we do have a good reason to be in the woods. Angie you spread out to me on the right. Catalina, on the left. Pace the others so they won't cross you. Go back when they go back. I will move the body farther out, maybe hide it."

The two women did as Hank instructed. It was not difficult to find. Hank had tracked wounded deer before. Finding a dead, bloody body in the woods directly in front of him was a piece of cake. There she lay, face up, if you could call it a face. It seems Catalina and Angie had continued to attack the corpse long after it had expired. Hank shuttered as he saw Tracy's crushed forehead, her right eye dangling from its socket, teeth smashed. There had been some hate in this doing.

Angie coughed, signaling that the others were going back. Hank began pulling the body northward. The woods ended into a meadow, yet he continued over the grass. Cresting a small rise, he pulled the body sideways and gave it a shove with his foot. The body rolled about ten feet downhill until its head struck a rather large rock with a thud. "Sorry about that," Hank whispered instinctively, then smiled at the ironic morbidity.

Hunter found himself still talking to Leroy, fascinated at the wisdom possessed by the simple man. The man had operated a greenhouse nursery. He was friendly, wise, and very amiable.

"Now me being here and meeting you might be just a coincidence, but it sounds like something more. I mean, I haven't been to Kansas City in thirty years. I am simply delivering rice to people in Harrisonville. Some National Guard armory there. I have 2000 lbs in the back of my truck. I was permitted 200 lbs for food and barter. I'm almost there, and I reckon you guys need the food more than I do."

God and Country

"So, did you pass anywhere near Middleton, Arkansas? My mom and her husband live near there. A place called Oak Grove."

"Son, I am from Oak Grove. At least that's where I moved after the DHS took over Middleton."

Hunter realized it was all making sense now. Then, slowly, expectantly, he asked Leroy: "Do you know my mom? Rebecca Hamilton?"

"No, I don't know any Rebecca Hamilton."

That confused Hunter a bit. He thought certainly...

"The only Hamilton I know was in the Army," Leroy interrupted Hunter's thoughts. "I doubt anyone will ever forget his name around my parts. Master Sergeant Jason Hamilton."

Hunter's mind grew numb. Jason Hamilton was his stepdad. He said so much aloud and, for the next hour, Hunter was in rapt attention as Leroy told him of how his stepfather had rescued the members of the 875th Engineer Battalion and their families, and how he had led an attack against a DHS headquarters.

Leroy placed his hand on Hunter's shoulder. "Son, your stepdad is a local hero. He and the mayor of Oak Grove sent me on this mission. This rice is a shipment to support the Missouri National Guard, our ally."

Hunter thought to himself. If his stepdad was safe, then most likely his mom and sister were, too. If there was one thing he knew for certain about Jason, he would give his own life to keep his wife and daughter safe.

"So, the way is clear all the way to Oak Grove?" Hunter asked.

"Clear is a bit of a stretch. The bridge at Black Rock on 63 is closed. I took the Strawberry bridge."

Hunter had no idea where that was.

"And there are some roadblocks on Highway 63 before I got to Hardy, but barring any DHS offensive, the way is mostly clear. I was in Oak Grove two days ago."

Two days. That is all it would take? Getting to Oak Grove had seemed like an impossible task.

God and Country

While Hunter was letting this settle in his mind, Angie walked up, looking very shaken and dead serious. Hunter turned to her excitedly, "Angie, I got some good news!"

Angie replied with a deadpan face. "Babe, I've got something to tell you as well."

―

"Well, we need diesel for the vehicle, that is for sure." It was 10 a.m., but still quiet, the refugees resting, twelve people per room. Hank nervously eyed two vultures circling the sky north of the motel. "It will take about two days for the caravan to reach Harrisonville on foot. I honestly don't think they have that much strength left in them."

"What about food? And water?" Angie asked. "For the refugees, I mean." Angie had tried not to let on about how shaken she was over yesterday's events. Catalina knew…because she had seen it; she was a part of it.

"We discovered another hot water heater used for the trucker shower area. Looks to be full, about 300 gallons."

"Too bad it is not hot water. I could go for a long shower," Catalina added, smiling at Hank.

"Yeah," Hank replied slowly, making eye contact and smiling. Then he looked away…

"We still have a little over 400 pounds of cooked rice. That might last them about a day and a half if rationed at two cups a day." Hank had seen the way the refugees had devoured the two cups of rice yesterday afternoon. A cup of rice was not a lot of calories, but it was better than nothing. "We can send a truck back," Hank added, trying to convince himself.

Hank had begun to regret that Leroy had left early that morning. 2000 pounds of rice was a lot. But not really. The extra food would simply delay the real problem: What does one do with three hundred people that need to be fed?

God and Country

The real answer became clear. Unless they were to abandon the refugees, all of the them would have to travel over thirty more miles to Harrisonville. Then, would the entire family serve as an advance party? No, someone would need to stay back with them.

"I will travel with them," Angie volunteered.

Catalina immediately responded, "If you are staying, I am staying. We will make that trip together." Hunter looked at Angie, Catalina, and Hannah, then back to Hank.

"Well hell, I guess we are all traveling together." Hunter shrugged his shoulders. There was an urgent need Hunter felt to find his mom, but there were also needs here.

"Jim, you were in the army, right?" Hunter inquired.

"A platoon sergeant in the National Guard."

"Well, we want you to take charge of this group."

"Where are you going?" Jim looked a bit concerned.

"No where. We will still be with the caravan, in back with the vehicle. But, we want you to lead the way. It is a tough job. Can you handle it?" Jim looked around at the people milling around outside. "You know you and your brother are the real leaders of this caravan, right?"

"We will still be here," Hunter paused. "For now… You can still come to us if you want advice. But you make the decisions."

"Okay."

"So then, what do we need to do to get these people ready to travel?"

"That is all the food we have?" Jim pointed to the office, where some 900 cups of rice had been prepared.

"That's it."

"And that tank we discovered yesterday?"

"Yup."

"I will need you to introduce me around so people know."

God and Country

Which is exactly what Hunter did. The refugees were called together. Hunter introduced the caravan to their new leader. Jim immediately took charge:

"Each of you are in a room. I want you to return to your individual rooms and vote for one leader for your room. Room leaders need to report back here to me in 20 minutes with four pillow cases."

Hunter looked at Hank. "We should have done this a long time ago." Hank nodded, and smiled. They went off to their room, following Jim's instructions. They had bunked with Jim's family, but Jim insisted that they also have a room leader. Besides, he wanted one of the brother's to be a close advisor.

"I nominate Hunter as room leader." Hank asked if there were any other nominations. No one spoke up. "All in favor of Hunter as room leader, say 'Aye." There was a resounding response. "Opposed?" Crickets.

"But why me?" Hunter pleaded, plopping himself on the bed. Honestly, Hunter was sick of so much responsibility.

"Maybe it is because you are the only one who knows where we are going," Angie smiled. Hunter took the pillow cases and went off to the meeting. Upon his return, the two families were outside the room, looking around. As Hunter walked to the room door, Angie stopped him. "Your brother and his woman needed some time." A few minutes later, Hank and Catalina opened the door. Hank wore the stoic face of some Viking warrior, not a hint of emotion. Catalina, however, was all smiles. As they walked past the families, Catalina patted Hank's butt. Angie beamed a radiant smile at Catalina, then winked.

Jim had room leaders collect three cups of rice for each room occupant and place it upon a large sheet of plastic wrap. The large ball of rice, about two and a half gallons on average, was placed in one of the pillow cases. That pillow case, and the three others were labeled with the leader's room number with a bright red Sharpie. All were given back to them.

God and Country

The next question Jim had to answer was how each room's team would carry water. Jim had addressed this problem with his team leaders while they were getting their meager food allocation. There were almost no closed containers in any building around. Hardly a single soda bottle. All had been scavenged.

Someone suggested they use the remaining plastic wrap. "It's going to get a hole in it, bust, or something." Another suggested using the steel containers used to cook. "It will slosh out before they walk two miles." The shower curtains? Maybe for a gallon but not twelve. As they were walking toward the truck stop parking lot, Hunter eyed something. A trailer load had been abandoned on the side of the road on the opposite side of the overpass. At first, it looked like lumber, but it had a different color. "That looks like pipe. Surprised nobody took them," Hunter whispered to another room leader.

"Yeah, well nobody wants new pipes when there is no running water," the other room leader replied.

"Okay, but pipes can hold water, right?" Hunter quietly suggested.

In the next hour, two room leaders were carrying four or five 3" PVC pipes back across the overpass. The pipes were plugged with paper and plastic, then covered with plastic wrap bound by string, twine, and bits of cloth.

"They seem to hold almost 6 gallons each," Jim replied. "Squad Leader Five, what is your name?" Jim had exchanged the words "room leader" with "squad leader." That change would stick.

"Jonathan Egerton," came the man's reply.

"Egerton, now that is what I call thinking outside the box. Outstanding!" Jim lavished the praise on the man. Few noticed that Egerton's eyes had uncomfortably shifted toward Hunter.

—

The convoy left that evening with each squad carrying a pipe full of water and about fifteen pounds of cooked rice. Jim explained to Hunter the reasoning behind splitting up the food and water. "If we need to abandon the highway, I want each squad to be somewhat independent. Each squad now has two firearms as well."

"Jim, just tell me what to do. You don't need to tell me why."

Jim looked at Hunter. "But we need you, sir."

The next day passed somewhat uneventfully. The caravan had been moving at night directly along the interstate. Each squad had chosen pairs of those who were able to carry the PVC water pipes on their shoulders. The 50 pound weights reduced their mass over that day, and by the second night's travel, the water pipes were abandoned and the food sacks had been emptied. The refugees were afflicted with a bone weariness that only time could cure. It was now their last evening of travel. With any luck, the caravan would make the National Guard post in Harrisonville before sunrise.

Jim saw lights at the overpass over a mile ahead. Traffic had been nonexistent for the most part along the interstate for a very simple reason, there was little fuel to be wasted. This probably meant it was military traffic. The question was "which military?"

"Contact left," Jim called out. The "squad leaders" repeated this down the line until it reached the hummer. Hank was amazed at the efficiency with which the weary caravan moved to the right and lay prone at the embankment of the road.

Hank turned the hummer off the side of the highway, the lights still in blackout drive. Hunter found an opening between small trees to the right of a small hill, and Hank, following the lead of his brother, drove over some small saplings, effectively disappearing into the dark vegetation. Hunter went back to the highway embankment and waited nervously with both his family and Jim's. Catalina and Angie held their rifles to front, in prone fighting position. Hannah lay next to Angie, imitating her adopted mother. Hank had lent the two pistols to Jim's wife and teenage son, while Hunter held his own M4. Counting Hank's M4 and .357, this squad, the last, was by far the most heavily armed. Jim had explained his reasoning to Hunter. He had required no one to give up any arms, and, if there were trouble, the hummer could act as an immediate reaction force to bring more

God and Country

firepower. What remained unsaid was that Jim wanted his own family well protected.

Hank ran down the embankment, leaving about fifteen of the weakest refugees with the vehicle.

"I reckon we might need these," Hank whispered to his brother. Reaching into his front jacket pocket, as if he were retrieving eggs, Hank carefully produced five M67 fragmentation grenades. He kept two for himself, then thinking again, gave two to his brother, then moved to give one each to Angie and Catalina. He had no idea if they were going to need them.

"Twist, pull pin, and throw. Only do that if you need to throw. And throw it far away at the bad guys." Lousy timing for giving a class on how to use a grenade, Hank thought.

"Like a baseball?" Catalina asked, her light Hispanic accent coming through.

"Yeah, like a baseball," Hank responded.

"Okay, baby." Catalina managed to plant a quick kiss on Hank's cheek. Somehow, even in the excitement of a possible gunfight, Hank managed to feel a bit embarrassed.

The oncoming vehicles were driving at full speed, then began to slow down as they approached the last of the hidden caravan. They had seen something. Hank looked over at Catalina. Her knuckles were white as she gripped the hand guards of the assault rifle. She looked at Hank with fear in her eyes. Hank, right beside her, returned her gaze.

"It's okay, Catalina." Then Hank added, "I love you."

Hank slightly lifted himself up when he heard the whistling brakes of the stopping vehicles. There was a HUMVEE, three large farm trucks, and an 8 ton troop carrier. Trying to get a good sight picture through his rifle sights in the near dark was useless. Looking above the rifle's rear sight aperture, Hank lined up the front sight to the rear of the troop carrier. He realized if the convoy had seen them, there was little hope. His family was with him, however, and he would fight like hell to defend them. He looked over at his brother. Hunter nodded that he was ready. Then the

God and Country

sound of a closing door. A passenger had gotten out of the hummer, walked down the embankment to where he was barely visible, and, after a moment, walked to the vehicle again. The convoy started to move down the road again.

    Hank felt like laughing out loud. Someone had stopped to take a piss. He turned over to Catalina, who had moved close to him. "Sometimes," Hank thought, "It takes the damnedest things to make you realize what is important." Hank looked into Catalina's eyes. They kissed.

Chapter 13

Rest

"Mr. Bowers told us you would be coming. We can use those who can hold a rifle." The commanding officer at the Harrisonville Armory wore the insignia of a major, but looked a bit young for that rank.

"But there are children here, and elderly," Jim interjected.

"Look, sir, what is your rank? Sergeant First Class?"

Jim nodded, "Yes."

"Well, shouldn't you be with your unit, sergeant?"

"Everyone in my unit is dead, sir."

"And you are the only survivor? Well, you will be attached to our unit. See the quartermaster, second building on the left."

"Sir, I am leading a caravan of three hundred refugees."

"That is not my concern. Again I say, I can accommodate those able to bear arms. No one else."

Hank, who was normally quite reserved, was becoming upset. He spoke up. "You have food, these people are hungry! Where is your fucking compassion?" Hank looked as if he were going to body slam the young major. Tension grew as the three enlisted soldiers in the room moved their rifles in the direction of the angry, young man. Instantly, Jim, Angie, and Catalina had drawn weapons, pointing them at the soldiers in what appeared to be a Mexican stand-off. Hunter put his arm around Hank's shoulder and his other hand on his brother's arm.

"And who might you be?"

Hank was not speaking. Hunter spoke for him. "This is my brother, Hank, my family…and let me suggest we all calm things down a notch." The major nodded, and the soldiers lowered their weapons.

"Major Putnam," the officer introduced himself.

Hunter nodded. The family reciprocally lowered their weapons.

"Sir," the major continued as if the near disastrous situation had never occurred, "Let me address the issue of compassion. We have a limited garrison of 117 personnel. I alone am responsible for the welfare of my men. I do my best to protect the southbound route against Federal incursion. We have limited resources."

"What about the 2000 pounds of rice Leroy brought you two days ago?" Hunter countered.

"Do you know how many days that will feed my men?" The major's voice took on a chiding, didactic tone.

Actually, Hunter had a very good idea how many days that would feed them. 2000 pounds of dry rice could produce approximately 15,000 cups of cooked rice. About 200 calories per cup. 5 cups of rice were not enough for military half rations. The refugees had consumed that little over a two day period. Now that he thought about it, Hunter could not fully explain how the caravan had managed their journey. This major was not showing any compassion, and Hunter was beginning to get angry himself. Losing control, however, would do nothing to feed the refugees, nothing to feed his family.

"Look at the refugees as an asset. Some of us have combat experience. Others are able to free up men at the garrison to help you out. If your only concern is the welfare of your men, you miss the bigger picture. Is your mission not to help out the people of this community?"

"My mission is dictated by the Missouri State Guard, recently relocated to Fort Leonard Wood. You, sir, have no idea as to my mission."

Hunter realized he was losing ground in the argument. Hunter tried to think. Suddenly, Hunter stated: "My stepfather, Master Sergeant Jason Hamilton of Oak Grove, Arkansas sent Mr. Bowers to you three days ago as an envoy. Do you think the family of a vital ally should be denied the very sustenance they have provided?"

The mentioning of Hunter's stepdad stunned the young major. He apparently recognized the name. Finally the major responded. "I will consult headquarters in regard to your request." Another pause. "Corporal, inform the Quartermaster to feed and house this civilian caravan." Then, to

God and Country

Hunter, "You may keep your arms, but please instruct your people to not stray from the barracks area, for their safety." Hunter nodded.

The mess section was preparing a meal of bean soup, cornmeal mush, and rice. It was more than Hunter had eaten in a week. His stomach had been so used to going without food that he was surprised how his stomach had started growling with the smell of it. He looked down at his own belly, at the weight he had lost over the last 8 months. How had the caravan, who had been mistreated in prison, managed to make the journey here? How had they not quit, fallen out from exhaustion, starvation? It had been nothing short of a …. "No, don't say it," Hunter told himself.

Jim had met with the twenty-four "squad leaders," instructing how they would divide their squads into two person teams, who would feed each other.

"You will take up all firearms from the squad. You will have a weapon at ready. You will divide up your squads in groups of two so they can monitor each other as they eat," Jim instructed the squad leaders.

"That is a bit much, don't you think?" one squad leader said. "You can't treat people like babies," another person commented.

"Yes, damnit, like fucking babies. Or would you have someone hurling their guts out, then continue dry heaving until they injure themself? We cannot be seen wasting food. We are at a precarious moment here, gentlemen. We cannot afford to make waves. Your squad will follow your orders, or they will lose their rations all together, and so will you. Is that understood?"

A murmur.

"Is that understood?!"

A general affirmation of agreement was heard throughout the squad. They left to instruct their squad on instructions about chow. Hunter remained behind.

Hunter spoke to Jim alone. "These people are starved. I get it."

"I know. I hope our people do," Jim replied.

God and Country

The head cook, a staff sergeant, was in charge of issuing the rations to the grateful refugees. Half cup rice, half cup mush, one cup soup. Nothing else for now. "And sip water. Plenty of this water." The cook pointed to three lister bags behind him. "Another late evening chow is scheduled for this evening at 1930…umm 7:30 pm."

The quartermaster, a Sergeant First Class Landers, was impressed with the organization of the people. The leader of each group, each with a firearm, was the last of the group to go through the chow line. The leaders sat with their group on the grass, slowly eating as they had directed their squad. Most everyone could not finish their meager meal quickly, others not at all.

Jim stood monitoring the some three hundred people with the quartermaster beside him.

"What is in the water?" Jim asked the sergeant.

"A blend of salt, potassium, and calcium. Replacing the electrolytes. I like the way you have these people organized, by the way."

"Didn't have much of a choice. We have so many weak with hunger. Many older people and kids. We have ten kids under three."

"How many people died on the way here?"

"Nobody."

"Nobody? No way. It has to be 50 miles to KC."

"It took four days. How we did it is beyond me."

"Jesus!"

"Dunno. Maybe." Jim had taken the quartermaster's mild oath as a simple question. "See that guy there?" Jim pointed to Hunter. "He is the one who really led us here. He rescued us from Subtropolis."

"Sub-what?"

"The underground storage system in KC. DHS were holding us there. That man freed all of us, with just a knife! It was surreal."

"My God…" the quartermaster muttered this time, more like a statement.

God and Country

"Yeah," Jim had lowered his voice. "Nobody says that out loud, though, probably because it sounds crazy. If there is a God, do you think he would take sides in a civil war?" Jim asked quietly.

"I'm not religious."

"I ain't either, but I know what I've seen," Jim remarked matter-of-factly.

Changing the subject, Landers remarked, "I like how you have everyone eating like this."

"It is extreme, I know," Jim replied. Most don't know that you can die from eating. I was stationed in Africa on a humanitarian mission. We saw something called 'refeeding syndrome.' It wasn't pretty."

"Africa, where at?"

"Liberia. SETAF."

"No way! I was there in 2003."

"Yeah, me too! Do you remember Captain MacDonald? Big head? Nobody could stand him…"

"Yeah, 'Watermelon Head!'…."

And so the two continued their conversation as though they were lifelong friends.

The late afternoon stretched to early evening, with some of the refugees showing signs of "refeeding syndrome." Angie had set up a temporary triage center with help of a corporal, an army medic who was more experienced at treating the symptoms of malnutrition than his years seemed to allow. Jim approached Angie, who gave him an update on the sick among the refugees.

"Two serious condition, seventeen stable. Ms. Betty, she is seventy-eight years old. She started having seizures, so we have her resting with an IV. Her heart rate has normalized, but she seems confused. We have a three year old boy, Michael, who can't keep anything down. Again, IV."

Corporal Trevino walked up, interrupting Angie. "We lost Ms. Betty. Cardiac arrest. Not like I've ever seen before, though. Normally, patients are in acute pain, unable to speak. Ms. Betty seemed rested and alert, yet perhaps a bit confused. Her heart rate had slowed and was

God and Country

regular, her blood pressure almost normal. She even spoke to me before she passed," Trevino paused. Then, as an afterthought, the young corporal continued. "She said, 'Tell him God is on our side.' At least she seems to have died peacefully, right?" Corporal Trevino offered in consolation.

Where Corporal Trevino missed any relevance to Ms. Betty's last words, Jim did not.

—

The family rested. Corporal Trevino insisted that Angie leave, rest, and recover. Angie argued that her skills were needed at the center, but it was like talking to a stone wall. Angie went directly to the quartermaster to appeal her case, but he simply put his hand on her shoulder and said, "Ma'am, get some rest, please." And so the next seven days were nothing but chow and rest, something the refugees slipped readily into.

Jim never told Hunter about Ms. Betty's last words. God? Until recently, Jim had not believed that God, or ghosts, or space aliens existed. There was no way Ms. Betty had heard Jim's conversation with Landers. Yet, Ms. Betty's final words, which declared God's existence as self-evident, answered Jim's question: "Tell him God is on our side."

Jim decided to speak with Hunter.

"So, how did you know how to find us last week?"

"The underground place by the water park?"

"Yeah."

"It's a long story."

"Yeah, I heard you say that before. We have time."

"I met someone that told me to go to Kannfield Stadium."

"You met a dead person."

"He told me in a dream." As if that made Hunter's statement more believable. Hunter continued, "But when he said what to do, it seemed to make sense somehow." Hunter had avoided saying a dead man had made him soup, as if that were the part that would somehow be considered over-the-top crazy.

"So it was a hunch?"

"I had been in an accident. Maybe I wasn't thinking straight. I didn't see any other option."

"And you dreamt of where to find your family?"

"No, I dreamt I would find them," Hunter paused. "If..."

"If what?"

Hunter wondered how to put the words. "If I was willing to go."

Jim looked at him blankly. Hunter could see he didn't get it.

Hunter tried to gather his thoughts. How could he explain what he had felt. Then he started again: "A few years back, we had a rope that hung out over the river. You ever swing out on one?"

"Like out over the water, to jump in? Sure."

"I remember how scary it was the first time I did it. I had to run, jump out, and grab that rope. I had no idea if it would hold me. I just had to go for it."

"Yeah."

"It felt just like that. It was scary just like when I jumped out on that rope."

Jim thought as if in study for a minute, then spoke up. "Do you still do that? 'Hope in a rope?'" Jim asked, smiling.

"Nope," Hunter responded back with a smile of his own. "Sometimes, I hope in a dope. After all, I wanted you to be our leader."

The two men both laughed.

Chapter 14

Battle

It was nine days before Major Putnam called for Jim, Hunter, and Hank.

"Gentlemen, as you might be aware, I was tasked to provide you and your group a courteous rest and recuperation. I trust the accommodations were to your satisfaction."

They certainly had been. The three guests affirmed such.

"I have heard from my command, and I now offer you an option: to freely go or to stay under certain conditions."

The three men listened quietly.

"First, you may go. I can provide another two days ration to your group, but no transportation or other supplies."

"And if we were to stay?" Hank questioned.

"Sergeant Jim...?"

"Hafferty."

"Sergeant Hafferty, you have indicated you have approximately one hundred eighty people under your command in reasonably fit condition."

"Yes, many are parents of young children."

"Indeed, and you have one hundred and fourteen personnel that are aged, infirmed, or children."

"Those personnel, as you call them, are our past and our future," replied Jim.

"If you stay, my proposal to your group is one that necessarily hangs on a mission. If that mission fails, I can no longer offer refuge here in Harrisonville. I can only share the details of this mission if you decide to participate. What is your decision?"

Jim, Hunter, and Hank conferred. When the three agreed, the major moved them to a second room where SFC Landers and several other soldiers and civilians were seated at tables. Some Hunter recognized, some he didn't. Three empty seats had been reserved. The table supplied with notepads and pens. An easel was centered at the front of the room. The major walked to the front of the room and introductions were made. Then the major presented the Operation Order. All present took notes.

Situation:
Enemy Forces: A company sized element of the 33rd Infantry division augmented by a platoon sized element of the 603rd MP Battalion out of Fort Leavenworth, Kansas have recently taken the railroad depot in Louisburg, Kansas. Five M2 Bradley fighting vehicles have been observed in the area. Composition of the fighting force will most likely include four platoons of infantry equipped with light machine guns and vehicle mounted M2 machine guns, although none have been observed. The units possibly will be supported by drone and Apache gun ships.

Friendly Forces: Two companies of the 223 BSB out of Lamar and Harrisonville, Missouri. These two companies will be augmented with local militia. The 331 BSB will be equipped with troop transport, limited machine gun capacity, and small arms. They will carry shaped charges and Composite 4.

Civilian Considerations: We have friendly forces at Deerfield Granary and the local area. Kansas Guardsmen are in the area awaiting coordination of the mission. Civilian losses may be acceptable to achieve the overall objective.

Detachments: Those not battle ready from the Harrisonville militia will stay in Garrison. In addition, consideration for parents with children under ten will be observed as much as possible.

Attachments: Two composite companies of the 203rd Engineer Battalion out of Nevada, Missouri augmented with militia from the local area. The 203rd is equipped with M113 troop transport, HMMWV, and troop carrier vehicles. They have been equipped with a limited number of Javelin missile systems, M2 and light machine guns, and small arms.

Mission: To destroy the bridges crossing the Marmaton River and assist in destroying enemy forces in areas south of the Marmaton River NLT 151700MAR2014. Assist in establishing a military footprint at Louisburg capable of defending against future enemy threats from the north. Assist in protecting future crop production. Assist in securing stored grain facilities along and south of the Highway 54 corridor.

Execution: Alpha Platoon of the 223 BSB will exit Harrisonville, Missouri and coordinate with Deerfield Granary NLT 051700MAR2014. Coordination will be made with any Kansas Guardsmen at that time. Coordination with 203rd Engineer Battalion will be made via radio for final time of attack NLT 101700MAR2014. 223 BSB out of Lamar as well as Bravo platoon of the Harrisonville unit will harass the enemy QRF in enemy garrison, coordinating with the 203rd on time of attack. Remaining 223 BSB Harrisonville platoons will eliminate enemy personnel in the vicinity of the Highway 69 and destroy the bridges crossing the Marmaton River using shape charges, detonation cord, time fuze, and igniters. Then the Harrisonville unit will combine with Lamar to suppress enemy garrison efforts. Appendix A will contain relevant coordinates.

After enemy forces have been destroyed, Lamar and Harrisonville companies will coordinate to secure 4 other bridges crossing the Marmaton River. (See Appendix A) Friendly forces will relieve you at these duty locations NLT 201700MAR2014.

Logistics: Rations, arms and ammunition will be carried via personnel. Resupply will occur near Louisburg enemy garrison. Secondary resupply will be at Deerfield Granary. (See Appendix A). Transportation will be organic. No refuel will be provided in the foreseeable future. There is no transportation or provisions offered to any EPW. Medical support will be provided by the 318th Medical Company out of Joplin, Missouri at Deerfield Granary and after Louisburg is secured, at the resupply location.

Battlefield command will be 203rd BN S3. Consult SOI in Appendix B for frequency and ComSec. Initial security challenge will be "Trigger." Password will be "Guard." See SOI for changes.
—

Questions were asked and answered. The caravan was to assist in the destruction of the Highway 69 bridge, and any retreating enemy forces. SFC Landers would complete explosive training and help locate bridge vulnerabilities. One parent from each family would be allowed to stay back to guard garrison and the adjacent interstate. All other people between the age of fifteen and sixty, an estimated 120 people from the caravan would support the Louisburg mission.

"So our caravan is providing the bulk of the Harrisonville task in this mission?" Jim questioned.

"Sergeant, I know this is a hodgepodge mission," the major offered. "We ourselves are brigade support units. Although many of us were deployed to Iraq, very few of us, twenty-eight to be precise, have actual combat experience. Your population of refugees are almost three times the number of my soldiers and have depleted almost a month of our rations in eight days. It is necessary to hold back half of my soldiers here to help defend this interstate and garrison, yet it is also necessary that we complete this mission. If we cannot secure the grain stores south of Louisburg, we will all starve within two months. Furthermore, if we cannot secure a good grain harvest, we all will starve by the end of this year."

"You mentioned that both Lamar and Harrisonville have limited small arms capacity. What did you mean by "limited?" Hank asked.

"Exactly that," the major responded. "Our unit has 117 soldiers. We have 127 M16A2 rifles, 20 attached grenade launchers, and only four M249 SAWs. We lost quite a few personnel and assets over the last eight months."

"We have less than forty firearms among us," Hank commented.

"Indeed, it seems we have twice as many capable personnel as firearms. We may need to "buddy up" on firearms. Not an ideal situation, I know. Reminiscent of the Battle of Stalingrad."

Hank wasn't a student of military tactics, but he had seen a movie about the battle. One soldier would carry a rifle, the next soldier would carry five extra rounds with instructions to pick up his partner's rifle when he fell. If Hank recalled correctly, the casualties of that battle were catastrophic.

Jim spoke, "You mentioned that the caravan would find refuge. How? Where?"

"The local farms are lacking much fuel. Until things change, good old fashioned manpower will assist in planting and harvest. We coordinate with the granaries and farmers in the local area. You will provide labor for the farms. In return, you will have food and shelter. No free lunch, but a chance to survive....Any other questions?"

"Yes, sir," Hunter spoke up. "You mentioned no provisions nor transportation of prisoners. Do you not want us to take prisoners?"

"These, sir, are trying times. DHS forces moved as far as Nevada last November. Have you ever asked what happened to Harrisonville's population, a town of 10,000? Because the citizens of this town had the temerity to resist the government's tyranny, all the families of this town were forced from their homes in the dead of winter. Do you think yours was the only caravan to come down this interstate? There were thousands that were forced from this town on New Year's Day. They were bound for the Arkansas border." The major paused, collected himself, then continued. "We don't know how many people completed the journey. Hundreds did not. Older men and women, children...left on the side of the road."

Indeed, people in the caravan had spotted a few dead bodies on their trek to Harrisonville. The refugees had simply averted their gaze as if looking over roadkill, their human nature not wanting to dwell on the subject of death. But hundreds? Hunter shuddered.

"We fought back, but at the time the government forces were too much. We retreated. Some ninety-six of us were captured and executed."

God and Country

The objective nature of the major's speech dropped. There was a quiver in his voice as he spoke the rest. "Burned alive." Another pause. The major moved closer to Hunter. There was a tortured mixture of anger and pain in the young major's eyes.

"You could hear them screaming!" The major shouted through tears. He became momentarily silent, realizing he had lost control. He adjusted his ACU jacket, looking down at it, recovering his composure. "So…we haven't the resources to facilitate prisoners. Enemy personnel will be offered no quarter," the major said with an absolute finality.

The briefing ended. The three walked outside.

Jim spoke first. "We have a lot to do. Let's get some rest."

The brothers each hugged their friend.

"Later."

"Yeah, later." Jim said wearily, feeling the weight of leadership. He walked away to the barracks.

"Do you think the major is sane?" Hunter posed the question to his brother.

"Do you think any of us are really sane any more? All the things that have happened? So many people dead? Seems the whole world has turned bad. Maybe the world is insane. And you? Having dreams and shit? Like that is not insane? And look what we end up doing. Even when we try to escape, look how we end up. It's like we are wearing t-shirts that say "Will Kill for Food" or something to that effect."

"Taking Louisburg at least is a good thing. Clear objective," Hunter offered, as if trying to convince himself about the mission.

"Yeah, you are right. Just let me know when you have a dream about it." The brothers laughed at what they did not understand and made their way back to the barracks.

Training for the mission took a week. Hank and Hunter, because of their combat experience and leadership, were chosen to be a part of the bridge team. Catalina was also on the bridge team, perhaps because of her relentless insistence to have the assignment. Seventeen other refugees would be a part of the bridge team as well. With them would be SFC

God and Country

Landers, their trainer, who divided the twenty people up into two person teams, each person being designated Alpha and Bravo. Each team was assigned a weapon, most being M16 rifles. Despite her protest, Catalina was not assigned to Hank. Her partner was a 56-year-old grandmother from Saint Joseph, Missouri. Hank was with a fellow in his late thirties. A banker by trade. The short, curly-headed fellow would talk incessantly about anything and everything.

Hunter was assigned the youngest of the refugees to take part in the mission, a boy who had turned fifteen two weeks before. The boy had bright red hair, freckles, and a pronounced stutter. Although everyone was thin, the boy seemed incapable of holding any extra weight on him at all. Sheer tenacity alone must have allowed the boy to make the trip to Harrisonville.

The first day of training consisted of basic demolition training, which everyone received.

"This is det cord. This is time fuse. Know the difference. Time fuse has yellow markings…." There would be followup demolitions training with Alpha members.

At the end of the day, the team was released. Hunter walked back with his young partner.

"I juu…stt wanted you to knnn…ow what an honor it is to be ass..assigned to yyyou." The young teen just beamed with admiration when looking at Hunter.

"Thanks, kid."

"Geoff…rey."

"Thanks, Geoffrey."

"You can ccc…count on mmme. We wwwouldn't be there if nnot for you."

"It's all good, Geoffrey." Hunter placed his hand on Geoffrey's shoulder.

The kid had been through a lot. His mom and dad had both been killed before he was captured. Supposedly, he had only started speaking again after the rescue in Kansas City. The two split up. Hunter walked up to his brother, who seemed to be muttering to himself, agitated.

Hank was shaking his head.

"What's wrong?" Hunter enquired.

"My partner. If that guy don't shut up, I will fucking kill him. I swear, I will put my knife through his skull," Hank said with convincing sincerity.

"Tough day at work, huh?" Hunter offered.

"Yeah."

"Hi, Baby," Catalina came up to her man, passionately kissing Hank while managing to grasp his buttock.

"Hi," Hank finally managed to whisper, still embracing his woman. It was evident to Hunter that Hank was completely head-over-heels in love with Catalina.

"For God sake. Get a room," Hunter protested.

"We've got one," Catalina quipped back. "It's just too crowded."

—

The next day's training consisted of weapons training, to include disassembly/assembly of the M16, proper aiming and firing techniques, immediate and remedial action for stoppages. Hank, Hunter, and four others found themselves assisting Landers in the instruction. The days after that consisted of constructing fighting positions, camouflage, challenge/password, basic first aid, and patrol signals. Then a thorough briefing over the mission. By the end of that afternoon, everyone on the team could repeat the mission in detail. Although some had trouble with map reading, most could repeat directions to significant locations. For the final two days, both Hunter and Hank were appointed as the two squad leaders. Those last days, the group's practiced and modified fire team maneuvers, but in groups of four due to the limited quantity of weapons. Landers was aware that he had older people in his group, people that could not take too many hard falls. He had to go slower.

"But when the bullets are flying, what would you rather have? A bruised knee or a sucking chest wound? Faster!"

God and Country

"When your buddy falls, help him if you can, but quickly," Landers exclaimed during training maneuvers. Then Landers pointed to Hunter. "You stay down." Landers pointed to Hunter and exclaimed to his young partner, "Leg wound, blood squirting! What do you do?"

"Pressure?"

"Don't ask me. Do it!"

Geoffrey scrambled to pack the wound and applied the field dressing.

"Not enough. What now?"

"Tourniquet!"

"Damned right! Use his belt," Landers exclaimed. "Now what?"

"I take the rifle and continue the mission!"

"Move!"

"Buddy moving!" the young teen cried.

The last morning, Sergeant First Class Landers pushed them hard. Landers reminded them of the importance of this mission as they practiced.

"Move like you don't want to starve!"

"There can be no failure!"

"Take the weapon and drive on." Landers reminded the team. "You have a mission to complete. Mission first, or we all die."

The training was as complete as it could be. Landers gathered his team together. "Squads, you have been briefed thoroughly about our mission. You have trained. Now let me tell you something not in training," Landers paused.

"Some of you will be wounded, some wounds are fatal, some will die. There is no escaping that. However, our mission is vital to our survival. The enemy may be better equipped, better trained, but we are fighting for what is right. We are fighting to survive. There can be no failure. Mission first. Do you understand?"

"Mission first!" came the response.

The squads were dismissed.

—

God and Country

Hunter had found a chaplain, but not a ring. So, instead, he had fashioned a ring out of baling wire, carefully wrapping one strand around the other, then measuring with the thickness of his pinky, closed the wire to form a circle.

There, in the barracks, sitting on a bottom bunk, were both Angie and Hannah. He knelt before them, holding them, realizing this might be the last night he ever saw them. Hunter took Angie's hand, still on both knees, and said to both of them: "Right here, I have more than any man could ever hope to ask for." Hunter then pulled out the ring and looked at Angie, "...but I'm still asking for one more thing. Angela Kay Lipton, will you marry me?"

Angie laughed out the answer through joyful tears. "Yes, yes!"

Hunter embraced his future bride and his excited young daughter.

That night there was a small ceremony. The next evening, the mission team left Harrisonville.

—

The 8-ton troop transport that carried Alpha Company slowly came to a stop. They had traveled no more than 6 miles. The rest of the way was on foot.

"Too close to the Kansas border," Landers explained. "Stick to the treeline. Parallel the highway. Deerfield is one mile west."

The people dismounted, moved in file on foot through the rolling fields south of Highway 54 at five meter intervals. The moon was near full and the starry night made navigation easy, but also made for possible observation from the road. Landers took care to avoid silhouetting the crest of the gentle hills, a route that nearly doubled that final mile. Hank lead his squad behind SFC Landers. As they neared the granary, something appeared to be wrong. SFC Landers and Hank could clearly see the lights of the granary were on. That made no sense. Landers immediately raised his palm to halt the squads. The sign was relayed back to the rear of the patrol. Something was moving ahead. Landers flattened his palm, and moved it to the ground. The two squads took to the ground.

Landers knelt. Waited. Then he spoke.

God and Country

"Trigger," Landers spoke in a loud whisper. Nothing.

"Trigger." A bit louder. Landers tensed up. Hank was next to him, moving his rifle to ready.

"Guard," came a faint reply. A shadowy figure moved forward.

"Sergeant Nixon, Alpha Company, 891st Engineer Battalion."

The young sergeant had a facial injury to his cheek, the blood shining a dark red against his black skin in the moonlight.

"Are you 223rd?"

Landers confirmed this.

"We ran into trouble at the granary. I lost a point man, and was damned near shot myself while approaching the facility. Took fire, broke left. Evaded behind this ridge when the Bradley appeared across the road."

"They were expecting you?"

"Seems so."

"The whole mission could be compromised."

Landers thought for a moment. "Did they further engage you after contact?"

The young sergeant shook his head.

Landers paused to think. "Maybe they didn't have enough personnel to follow you, even with the Bradley. Their garrison is sure to be alerted to the contact, however." Landers thought he could make out the tracked vehicle under the trees along the road.

Landers reached to his LCE and took out a radio and notified the Nevada unit command about the possible mission compromise. The far end acknowledged, telling Landers to stand by.

Landers turned back to Nixon. "Sergeant, what are your assets?"

"10 personnel, two wounded, one ambulatory, one serious condition, all with individual weapons, but pretty low on ammo, sergeant. Two AT-4s."

"Ammo we have." Landers had limited weapons, but twice the ammunition combat load.

"...but an AT-4 won't cut it against a Bradley," Landers continued matter-of-factly.

God and Country

Landers had his two squads take up fighting positions, forming a perimeter. Then, Landers called in his second squad leader.

Landers explained the situation. Then he entertained thoughts.

Hank spoke up. "You mentioned not enough personnel to pursue. How many people are we talking about and what do they have?"

Landers spoke up. "I know the assigned crew of a Bradley is three, the commander, the driver, and the gunner. It can hold seven more."

Sergeant Nixon spoke up, "The armor squad normally has a grenadier and a soldier with anti-armor."

"Javelin?" Landers asked.

Nixon nodded.

"We can't outgun a Bradley, that is the problem."

"If we put a shape charge under it, that might create quite the headache," Hank offered.

"Maybe, but I don't think we can get that close. It would be a suicide mission for whoever tried," Landers countered.

"We can come in using the silos as cover," Nixon offered.

"Nixon, you mentioned anti-armor. Javelin. That is outside the vehicle, right?"

"Of course. Having it in the track would be defeating the purpose of having it," Nixon responded.

"If we get that, we can take out the Bradley, right?" Hank was following along.

"Possible. They would have an LP/OP. Fighting positions along the road, the Javelin would probably be there. They are bound to have a sniper. I would place him on top of a silo," Landers thought out loud. He continued in a monotonous low voice. "Yeah, we might be able to take out the sniper. But, the Bradley commander would instantly report it to their garrison. Win the battle. Lose the war. Not an option."

Hank continued, "We have an AT4, right?" He looked to Landers for confirmation.

"Again, the AT4 would be totally useless against the Bradley." There was a slight agitation in Landers voice. "It would be a spitball."

God and Country

"But would it take out the Bradley's antenna?"

That was something of which SFC Landers had not thought.

"We need recon. See if we can observe positions."

The next afternoon, they executed their plan.

An explosion hit the Bradley. On queue, Geoffrey raised a helmet on a stake. A metal can lid secured inside the camouflage band, which reflected in the afternoon sun. The kevlar helmet was knocked from the wooden stick and ten feet back as Hunter heard the shot go off.

"Got him?"

Hunter scanned forward, looking for the signal. "No, try again, at the second position."

—

From Hank's squad position off the south side of the highway, about a hundred meters from the granary entrance, Hank observed a soldier running from a fighting position on the opposite side of the road. The soldier crossed without any resistance and ran back toward the Infantry Fighting Vehicle. "See that?" Hank pointed to where the soldier had emerged. "One of their fighting positions. Place intermediate fire on that fighting position."

Another soldier ran from the position Hank had indicated. His squad opened fire. That soldier crossed the road and was going to drop near the culvert when his movement was terminated by a 5.56 round punching a hole through his left lung and devastating his liver. He suddenly went down on the edge of the road, with only his helmeted head succeeding in reaching the culvert.

—

On the woodline south of the granary, Hunter could hear a staccato cacophony erupting on the road. Geoffrey held the helmet up on a stake a second time. This time a round knocked the helmet in two distinct pieces. The sniper was good.

Suddenly came the deafening drone of 25 millimeter rounds. The Bradley's chain gun had not found the refugees closest to them, a mere thirty yards from the vehicle. Instead, the vehicle's gunner had targeted

God and Country

Hunter's rearward position. The rise of land that had been providing cover was being plowed by a gun designed to penetrate a foot of armor. Hunter instinctively closed his eyes tightly, covered his ears with his hands as he attempted to become one with the ground. He could hear the larger trees being splintered, the smaller trees being mown down. Was this it? After all he had seen? The end? Angie would raise Hannah. God, let them be okay. Just as suddenly as it began, the exploding, murderous assault paused, then shifted below...

Unheard by Hunter, his squad positioned below him had seen the sniper atop a grain bin and was firing upon his position. It was perhaps not the most accurate fire considering the eight militia were novices, but accurate enough to cause the sniper to move toward cover.

This was what Landers was waiting for. Landers had managed to move the team of Kansas guardsmen around to the other side of the granary. Their goal was to take out the sniper and lure the Bradley to engage them. The Bradley's thunderous weapons fire did not distract Landers from his mission. Landers identified the sniper's location on top of the leftmost grain bin, and waited until the sniper worked his way around the top rail. The thunder of gunfire paused. Landers took aim and fired once, then again. The sniper dropped on the top rail of the walkway, balancing lifelessly some forty feet in the air.

Around the other side of the grain bins, the track gunner had taken a moment to identify and acquire the new target just a few yards away. Realizing the danger to her squad, Catalina made an instant decision to lead her fellow squad members in a mad rush forward, seemingly to assault the tracked vehicle. The track gunner opened up the 7.62 coaxial machine gun, dropping three refugees as Catalina led the squad in a rush past the Bradley, between two of the huge cylindrical bins.

Landers saw the refugee team through the bins, and expected the vehicle's destructive guns to tear through the storage buildings' metal shell like paper. But no, instead, he heard the diesel engines rev up. The vehicle was purposely avoiding the grain bins as targets and was coming around.

God and Country

Hank was moving with half his squad while the other maintained covering fire on the known fighting position. Shouldn't there be another fighting position on this side of the highway? A 5.56 Squad automatic weapon spoke up directly ahead, answering his question. His partner shuttered in response, stopping, and dropping down. Hank dropped in front of him, then wormed his way back to him. The irritating, bald little man looked at Hank and issued one last rasp of breath. A final, unintelligible thought? It no longer mattered.

"Okay, okay," Hank thought. He grabbed his single grenade. Then, in realization, searched his partner's jacket pockets and produced a second one. Twist, pull pin. Lever fall. One thousand one, one thousand two. Throw up. Take cover. An air burst. That might buy him a second or two. A second twist, pull pin. This time he rose up on his knees and made an aimed pitch. His mother always said he would have been a good baseball player, and her words were justified with a throw accurate enough to make any major league catcher nod in respect.

Hank lifted himself up. Two of his team members moved forward and into the destroyed fighting position, arming themselves with two undamaged weapons inside the foxhole. The team then turned their attention to the fighting position across the highway, providing a devastating crossfire.

"Okay, back to the plan," Landers thought to himself as the armored vehicle rounded the corner. "Run!" Landers took off. His job was to be bait for a twenty-five ton death machine. Catalina and most of the squad made their way to the cover of the drainage ditch at the side of the road, but two squad members ran the same direction as Landers. As the vehicle rounded the grain bins, the coaxial machine gun opened up in the drainage ditch. Landers found himself literally waving his hands in the air, running backwards as he neared a pile of gravel at the edge of the loading area. The turret swung around, the coaxial opened up again, and two refugees dropped, hit by the 7.62 mm rounds targeting them.

"Come on, come on," Landers lifted himself up, then hit the ground as rounds exploded in front of him, sending fragments of gravel all around. "And now!"

Sergeant Vickers could not hear SFC Landers yell out, but he had been watching the chase from the drainage ditch. In his hand he held two M60 igniters. One had a white string tied on the ring. He pulled that ring.

A one pound brick of C4 exploded on the left side of the approaching tracked vehicle. The driver of the vehicle instinctively swerved to the right, driving toward what appeared to be a log. It actually was a concealed shape charge. Vickers pulled the second ring as the right front track was bearing down on the explosive.

The Bradley track was thrown. A Kansas guardsman ran from his position and up on the disabled vehicle. The Bradley revved its engine, moved forward, and shed the right track. The guardsman held on to the entry hatch handles while the vehicle circled ninety degrees right. Then the vehicle stopped, and the gun turret began to pivot, but not before Vickers jumped on the vehicle, holding a rock. He banged the rock against the vehicle.

"We have a shape charge up here. Come out or we will test your hatch covers free of charge!"

The turret stopped turning.

Vickers pulled the cigarette butts out of his ringing ears. Probably would have some hearing damage but nothing like the occupants of the armored vehicle underneath him. The hatch cover opened. Out emerged three infantrymen, hands-up, noses bleeding.

"They probably have concussions," Landers thought as he came up from behind the gravel pile and moved toward the disabled vehicle. Then a shot rang out, and Landers fell.

Meanwhile, back on the road, the two soldiers in the remaining enemy fighting position had tied a brown t-shirt to the butt of a rifle and were waving it, when two large explosions behind them at the grain bins caused them to drop back in their foxhole. Hank ran over to the other side

God and Country

of the road and aimed his rifle. The two soldiers got back up, and Hank had them exit their position. He waved his squad forward toward the grain bins, leaving two refugees to watch the two infantrymen prisoners lying prone on their bellies.

Hunter and Geoffrey had moved out of their fighting position and toward the grain bins as well, when they heard the explosions. First, from the highway, then a moment or two later, two massive blasts. Running down the slope, they moved toward the large storage buildings. On the outside of the leftmost bin, an enemy soldier was aiming a weapon, firing.

Hunter aimed his rifle and fired a three-round burst. At least two bullets hit their mark. The soldier fell. Hunter ran up to the dead soldier and pointed to the M4 laying on the gravel. Geoffrey grabbed the weapon up and ran around the bin. They rounded the corner to find militia and guardsmen aiming weapons their way. A surprised militia member, a quite pretty woman in her forties, fired a shot at them, ricocheting off the corrugated steel surface of the grain bin just inches from Hunter. Realizing who it was, the woman looked abashed, and hung her head down.

Hunter and Geoffrey ran over to Landers, who was lying on the ground. It was a wound to the lower leg, just above the knee. Geoffrey applied immediate pressure and yelled to Hunter: Get his www…web bbelt! Need a ttt…tourniquet!"

"Wounded. We have wounded," Hunter yelled to his squad, pointing behind the bin. Hank pointed to the driveway. Hank's squad had fanned out to form a perimeter. SGT Vickers had taken his guardsmen to sweep the area for further threats

---

That afternoon, the losses were tallied.

"Counting previous losses, five dead, seven wounded, including you." Hank felt the numbers did not do justice to the loss.

"Jesus," Landers muttered. "Enemy?"

"No resistance. Five dead, 5 prisoners."

"Weapons and ammo?"

God and Country

"We have a net gain of weapons. Our gains are..." Hank consulted his list: "One 5.56 SAW, seven more rifles, two pistols, a Javelin, and 16 hand grenades. 2000 rounds of cased 5.56 and 24 40 millimeter grenades. 12 HE and 12 AB."

"Good job, Hank." Sergeant Landers seemed happy at that news, silently noting the grenades would greatly increase their M203 capacity. "Any grenade launcher?"

"Not operational. The 203's tube and two rifles were seriously damaged in a grenade explosion."

Sergeant Vickers spoke up, "Sergeant Landers, I think I can get that Bradley somewhat mission capable."

"Explain," Landers said tersely, biting down his lip in an evident attempt to fight off a wave of pain. Blood clot and pressure had later stopped the bleeding, but not the pain.

"The track is thrown. That is operator maintenance. The basic Issue Items have all the tools I need. We have three shoes to replace what is damaged. I think we can get it moving."

"You said somewhat mission capable."

"The front sprocket wheel has a broken tooth. That would make it non mission capable in garrison, but you can circle X that. You just might be more prone to slip the track again if you turn too fast."

"How long will it take? We have to get moving. Someone we don't want to see is bound to check up on us."

"I can break track with what I have. Piece of cake. Thirty minutes."

"Get on it."

"You, Sergeant Landers," Hunter interjected, "...are not going any where. You can't move."

"No shit. But with an operational Bradley, two tow missiles, and a Javelin, the tactical advantage might have shifted slightly in our favor," Landers said, in obvious pain.

"Considering it seemed pretty much a suicide mission before, any change is welcome."

God and Country

"Leave a detail of two back to care for the wounded."

"What about the prisoners? We are not going to kill them. We are not evil," Hunter remarked.

"Yeah, you are right. Okay, leave four. I will call for a medic as well. We need a new battle plan. Hank, you will be in charge."

The brothers nodded.

"And...we could use the prisoners' uniforms."

After the three remaining 223 platoons arrived, Landers began the briefing. Jim was present with two soldiers and a civilian, all of whom Hunter recognized from their earlier briefing.

"So if I understand this, we are hoping to use the element of surprise using enemy uniforms and the dead as a ruse," Hank summarized.

"But how did you get the challenge and running password?" Hunter asked.

"Let's just say I convinced them." Hank thoughtfully had taken out his hunting knife and was cleaning his nails.

Hunter understood, then he spoke up. "Jim, Sergeants Ealey, Travis, Mr. James, and I will draw out enemy forces on the eastern flank, falling back to the other side of Highway 69." Jim nodded.

"Correct. When in position, the 203rd will flank from the south.

It was 5 a.m. when Sergeant Vickers drove the Bradley slowly down the road.

"Okay, Hank, you are up."

Hank nodded and readied himself for the performance.

He knew the names of the enemy dead. Even a nickname. The active duty company would certainly know each other. Probably the MPs attached would recognize all their soldiers as well. Hank had to distract them.

Hank opened the hatch and raised himself. The track slowed even further as it approached the sandbagged guard shack.

God and Country

"Vanguard," Hank almost shouted the running password. "Vanguard!" Even louder. A spotlight came on opposite the guard shack, illuminating Hank.

"Identify yourself."

"You know fucking well who we are." Hank spoke with an indignant voice.

"They killed Sergeant Ski, Corporal Hanson, and Anderson." Hank pointed to one of the bodies on the front of the vehicle. "Frogger and Aimes are in the back. Grenades. Took out our comms, too. Now lose the fucking light and let us through." Hank hid his face, pretending to shield his eyes from the bright light. "Frogger is bad off."

The sentry waved off the light and let the tracked vehicle pass, yelling to Hank, "We called and let Gentry know you are coming. He's still in the cafeteria. Pull right up. Then move online for general stand-to."

In the predawn darkness, Hank gave the guard a thumbs up and rolled forward.

—

Over her protest, Catalina and her partner were assigned to medical, along with another buddy team. They had lost another militia, a school teacher from Hunter's squad. An abdomen wound had proved a slow, painful death. Still, Catalina kept a brave face while caring for the injured woman. When the teacher passed, Catalina cried.

In front of her, against a silo wall, sat six enemy soldiers, hands behind their back, zip-tied hands and feet…in their underwear.

—

"There is not a plan for small shit like this," Hank thought as his Bradley approached the repurposed school campus. "Gonna need to wing it." The cafeteria entrance had been blacked out for light discipline. As Hank approached, he noticed an observation post some 50 feet in front of the building. As he passed in the darkness, he called out, "Hey guys, we need all the help we can get." In response, the silhouette of a soldier left the post following them.

God and Country

"Gentry! We need two stretchers! Four wounded, two ambulatory!" Hank yelled after shutting down the Bradley's Cummins engine.

A person at the cafeteria door called back into the entrance for more help. Four soldiers bearing stretchers. "Help extract our wounded," Hank ordered the approaching guard.

"Clear the door!" The door lowered, and out exited two soldiers to make way for the aid. Gentry made his way forward to the dim red light of the Bradley, designed to preserve night vision. Two casualties were laying on the floor half on top of the others in the cramped space of the personnel carrier. "Give me a hand moving these guys, careful."

The two non ambulatory casualties were carefully moved, with one of Hank's crew maintaining pressure on a casualty's wound. There was quite a surprise when the "injured" patient shoved a gun in Gentry's neck.

"You aren't Frogger."

"No, I'm Shut the Fuck Up." Behind the litter bearers, two of Hank's crew lifted rifles, prodding their new captives.

Hank jumped down from the Bradley to the captives and simply stated, "I can either gag you or slit your throats. I can live with it either way. You can't." He pulled out his hunting knife. "Understand?"

Gentry nodded quietly.

"Good."

Another of Hank's squad made his way to the observation post and entered. Too late, the guard recognized the threat. Having the momentum, the militiaman dispatched the sentry with a seven-inch stiletto in the guard's liver.

Back at the Bradley, the prisoners were disarmed; their hands were zip-tied behind their backs. Gags had been fashioned from the captives' field dressings and wrappers.

Hank spoke quietly to their prisoners, "Gentlemen, you have no idea how lucky you are to be sitting this one out." The prisoners were placed inside the tracked vehicle, their feet being zip-tied as well.

God and Country

Six members of Hank's squad took up three positions among the evergreen landscape in front of the school. Hank heard other tracked vehicles firing up. Soldiers were moving more inside the building. The stand-to. Hank mounted his vehicle, tied something on the outside of the hatch, then buttoned up and looked down to Sergeant Vickers. "Are you ready?" Sergeant Vickers gave a thumbs up.

Outside the tracked vehicle, soldiers of the 1st Infantry Division began running out various entrances in the increasing dawn light. Vickers slowly drove the Bradley to align abreast of three other tracked vehicles emerging from between the main building and a school annex.

Positioned across the four lane highway from the enemy garrison, Hunter had both his militia and the Kansas guardsmen positioned south, on the left flank of the larger Harrisonville unit. Their position was on the east side of Highway 69. He was able to watch with amazement at how easily Hank's squad had managed their way through the guard post. He took a partial view of four tracked fighting vehicles positioning themselves on the greenery of the school's lawn. Soldiers were walking behind the Bradleys, with some moving to fighting positions about fifty yards in front of the school house.

"Wwwhich one is Bb...Hank?" Geoffrey was really starting to grow on Hunter.

"His will be the tank that starts shooting the other tanks." Hunter grinned.

"Oh."

Hunter took a closer look. Through the dim early morning light, he thought the leftmost Bradley had a white sheet attached on top.

Jim came running from the north. "Okay, we pop the high explosive first. Then engage with the grenade launchers, like mortars. Hit to the back and sides of the tracks. Things will heat up when the 203rd units flank."

"See that flag? That's Hank."

God and Country

Jim gave a glance with his field glasses. "I will try to inform Nevada after I pop this party off."

Hunter nodded, realizing the 203rd had Javelins. Tank killers.

—

Hank heard the explosions. The dull "tinking" after each explosion confirmed that the Harrisonville unit was using antipersonnel grenades. A Bradley's 25mm Bushmaster opened up in response, targeting across the highway, then another. That was his cue to attack the other tracked vehicles. Hank himself took control of the vehicle.

"Target the closest Bradley, TOW missile," Hank yelled.

"Roger, targeted," Vickers responded, grinning.

"Fire."

"TOW away."

The missile struck the Bradley directly in the side. A vicious blast was immediately felt by Hank, seeming to penetrate the armor of his own vehicle. "No wonder," Hank thought. "The exploding vehicle was only 50 yards away."

Hank drove around the smoking vehicle, which was obviously disabled. He was hoping that no other vehicle saw what occurred. Another Bradley came into view.

"Got it, Vickers?"

"I got it."

"Fire."

—

Eight dismounted members of Hank's armor squad, who had taken positions by the school's main building, had begun firing upon the enemy soldiers to their front, creating a crossfire for the enemy infantrymen. A wave of infantry reinforcements, however, were beginning to run from where the Bradleys had first appeared. The Kansas guardsman manning the left flank, responded by traversing his SAW west, firing at the reinforcements. It was looking grim for him to hold his position, when the second Bradley exploded in a deafening roar.

God and Country

Then another Bradley turned and started making its way back toward the school building, right back to him. The guardsman realized there was no use firing his 5.56 millimeter machine gun at the armored vehicle. The Bradley then began moving in his direction, firing its 7.62 coaxial machine gun.

Hank, realizing he was out of missiles, turned immediately toward where the enemy tracked vehicles had come. Vickers, manning the Bradley's weapons system, was targeting a rather large group of infantrymen running up the drive between the two buildings with his machine gun. "Two enemy APCs left," Hank thought. Somewhere behind him, Hank heard a large explosion. "Maybe one?" He slowed his track as he made his way up the drive, allowing Vickers to more accurately target the enemy. There was not much of a fair contest between infantrymen and a Bradley Fighting Vehicle. However, war was seldom fair. Hank moved the track forward, searching for the fifth tracked vehicle, needing to find it. That enemy track's Bushmaster gun would tear through Nevada's M113s and their light armor. Hank had to do something.

Hunter witnessed as Jim deployed his one Javelin against the remaining Bradley Fighting Vehicle, watching the Javelin missile lift up, then forwarding its destructive mass into the remaining enemy track. The Bradley was effectively turned into a burning metal wreck. Jim's troops continued to use their grenade launchers as mortars, raining down deadly fragments on the enemy. With the destruction of the 3rd Bradley, however, the Nevada battalion began their own assault from the southern flank with their M113 troop carriers. The M113's had been in hiding, being no match against the superior tracked vehicles, but with that threat seemingly eliminated, the dated armored transports moved forward against light infantry out in the open. The light APCs moved slowly forward, with members of the 203rd using the tracks as cover. They trod their way onto the campus grounds, effectively suppressing their antagonists with .50 caliber machine gun fire. Grazing crossfire came from the main building as

God and Country

well. Enemy soldiers who had been in the open were either dying or finding cover in their two tiered trench defenses and fox holes. Jim called the 331st to advance, moving across the highway toward the beleaguered defenders, who found themselves assailed on three sides. Having crossed the highway, Hunter could see some enemy troops attempting to surrender, hands up. They were shot dead. No quarter was being offered to enemy troops. They were going to slaughter them!

—

Hank had turned north around the main school building, to see the remaining enemy fighting vehicle making a left turn ahead. He could not let that remaining Bradley engage their troops. Hank accelerated the large vehicle.

"How can you stop that track?" Hank yelled above the engine noise to Vickers.

"Hit its track with the Bushmaster."

"Do it. Hold on!"

The Bradley made a turn at 35 miles an hour, losing the road, spinning a little in the lawn as it regained its traction. Vickers opened up the vehicle's main gun with a droning roar.

—

Hunter had dropped his M4 carbine and found himself running onto the school yard. He had no idea what he was going to do. He did know, however, that slaughtering surrendering soldiers was wrong. There was another roar of heavy gunfire, from where he did not know. More grazing fire. Enemy soldiers were being slaughtered. Running out toward the oncoming M113 tracked vehicles, Hunter began crossing his arms as he ran in a sort of cease-fire motion. Bullets flew around Hunter, seeming like rain.

—

"What the hell is Hunter doing?" Jim thought to himself. "Cease fire! Cease fire!" Jim frantically moved his hand across his face to the skirmish line of his attacking unit.

God and Country

Hunter veered left and ran directly in front of the lead M113, which incredibly came to a slow stop. The commander of the vehicle, a young captain, raised from the hatch. "What the fuck are you doing?" Are you fucking crazy?" he yelled.

"Is he fucking crazy?" It was as if Jim had heard the young track commander. Jim signaled the 223rd to stop. Jim put an outstretched hand above his eyes, then pointed to himself. WATCH ME. Jim moved forward, alone, toward the enemy position.

"These soldiers are surrendering," Hunter responded loudly. Weapons fire on the field had stopped. There was both an eerie silence and echoing gunfire ringing in Hunter's ears.

"We have orders to take no prisoners," the captain countered.

"That is an unlawful order, Captain, and you know it." Hunter had climbed up the side of the tracked vehicle.

"Do you know the things they have done to us?" the captain asked Hunter incredulously.

By now, the members of the 223rd had made their way to the enemy positions, following Jim's lead. They began accepting the enemy combatants as prisoners, taking their weapons. Hunter climbed the M113 to better address the vehicle commander.

From the south side of the school, a Bradley appeared with Hank sitting atop the main gun turret. Every soldier on the field momentarily stopped and looked Hank's way as he lifted his hand to greet his brother. Soldiers made way as Hank's vehicle rolled its way close to where Hunter stood.

Then Hunter spoke to the captain, "I know what the government has done. They raped and killed my wife." Mentioning it still brought tears to Hunter's eyes. Then Hunter raised his voice, addressing everyone present.

"Someone has to stand for what is right. These soldiers," Hunter pointed to the prisoners in front of them, "...are not our enemy; they live here. They have families here. Damn it, some of them are die-hard Kings fans!" Hunter gestured through his tears.

A few smiled and nodded, in a concession of sorts.

Hunter continued, "But we must stand for what is right..." Hunter paused. "...if for no other reason, then because no one else will!"

"But, we need to protect our families," a Nevada guardsman offered a protest.

"Yeah, we do." Hunter looked down, thinking about Hannah, and about his family. Then he looked up again. "But if we do something so evil today, how could we ever forgive ourselves, much less our children? How could God ever forgive us?"

There was a murmuring. A sense of agreement.

"And what are you gonna do?" the young captain said bitterly. "What can you do if we just finish them off right here?" the captain said with a determination bent on evil intent.

"Then you will have to deal with me," Hank's booming voice seemed to carry in the wind. Hank tapped the Bradley's turret, which shifted slightly in effect.

"And you will have to deal with us," Jim and several others had moved behind Hunter.

―

Later that night, in private:

"What the hell did you do today?" Hank asked his brother, incredulously.

"We did what was right."

"Yeah, but you jeopardized our place in Harrisonville. You heard Major Putnam. No prisoners."

"Remember when the DHS agents murdered that family in the field? Remember how they murdered Pastor John? We don't do that."

Hank remembered. It seemed like a long time ago. Had it only been seven months?

"They are people. Maybe they did wrong in the past. They can choose to do right. They can change."

"Did you have another dream?"

"No." Hunter thought about it. "It just seemed the right thing to do."

"I got your back, brother." Then, a long silence.
"What do we do now?" Hank finally asked.
"I have no idea."

―

"Sergeant Hafferty, I gave you a direct order that there would be no prisoners." The major was infuriated.

"I couldn't follow that order," Jim countered. "It wasn't a lawful order. If I followed that order, I would be guilty of murder."

"Sergeant Landers. What have you to say of this?"

"Sir, I wasn't there." Indeed, Sergeant First Class Landers was in a wheelchair with his right leg elevated. Where Geoffery had been able to save Landers' life, it was still questionable whether the corporal would be able to save his leg.

"So you took it upon yourself to change the order given to you, Mr.... Hunter?" The major had not seen fit to learn Hunter's last name, and that failure mattered not a wit to Hunter.

"The entire plan changed, sir." Hunter remained silent for a moment, then spoke further. "But, even if we had not been forced to change the plan, I wouldn't murder people in cold blood."

The major was incensed beyond words for a moment. Finally, the officer found speech again. "Sergeant Landers, arrest these three militia for dereliction of duty. Immediately!"

"I can't do that, sir. Hunter is right. You were wrong, sir." Landers spoke the truth, the order was not legal. There was another reality that Landers had to consider as well, however. Although Landers was not there to see it himself, the men of the Harrisonville battalion had witnessed something. They had seen an unarmed man run into heavy gunfire, a literal firing squad, without a single wound. They had seen that man stop a raging battle. How that had happened was seemingly inexplicable. One thing was certain, however, no one in the 223rd would lift a finger against Hunter, nor his brother.

"Corporal, arrest these men!"

God and Country

The corporal did not need to look to Sergeant Landers for advice. He had been at the Battle of Louisburg and seen what had happened yesterday morning.

"Sir," Sergeant Landers addressed the major. "I am placing you under arrest for violation of the Law of War, Article 2, Clause 2 of the UCMJ. Sergeant Hafferty, Corporal Napier, would you assist me in this detention?"

"You will not get away with this mutiny! I will…"

"Sir, you have the right to remain silent," Landers responded. "Gentlemen, please escort the major to the confinement facility."

Landers remained behind. "I now have an extra one hundred and forty-seven prisoners. What am I to do with them?"

"Have you considered letting them help with the planting and farm work?"

"Prison labor?"

"Perhaps they will realize that our cause is a just one. Who knows. Have some faith."

—

The two brothers walked back to the billets. There had been casualties, there were tears. Making their way to their bunks, Hunter was met by his new bride and daughter. Tears of joy were in their eyes as they held Hunter. Hunter was damn thankful to be alive and see his girls.

Hank held Catalina in his arms. He looked into her eyes. "You know, I almost lost you back at Deerfield. I realized I never want to be without you." Hank sat Catalina down on the lower bunk. "Catalina Sanchez, will you marry me?"

The next day there was a wedding. Dressed in a pair of military trousers and a OD green t-shirt, Catalina was nevertheless radiant. Hannah had made Catalina a tiara woven of clover flowers. It was a good ceremony.

Hunter could not help but notice how beautiful his wife looked as she watched the wedding couple exchange their vows.

God and Country

"Beautiful, isn't it," Hunter stated, unable to keep his eyes from the radiant beauty beside him.

"Babe?" Angie looked up at her husband, "I'm pregnant."

Hunter couldn't rid himself of a rather stupid-looking grin for the rest of the day.

And then came the goodbyes.

Hank and Hunter shook Sergeant Landers hand. Jim would take nothing less than a hug.

"Brother, we are going to miss you," Jim told Hank.

"Who knows, we may be back this way. Hopefully, those farms will take off."

"You betcha."

Jim turned to Hunter and just stared for a moment.

"What the hell are you looking at?"

"You know we need you here," Jim confided.

"Bud, this is where you belong, but we have to get to our family."

"Okay." The two hugged.

With their vehicle packed, the family turned to get in the hummer. Suddenly, Geoffrey came running up. "Hunter." His stutter was getting better.

Hunter turned around. He saw the smallish red-headed teen standing in front of him. "I'm g…going to tell everyone about what h…happened. I'm gonna write your story."

"You do that, kid." Hunter placed his hand on the teen's shoulder. "Just do that."

Hunter turned and walked to the hummer, and got in the front passenger seat to ride shotgun.

"So what now, brother?" Hank looked over from the driver's seat.

"We find mom," Hunter met his gaze.

"And after that? Are you going to start a church or something?"

"Naw," Hunter smiled and replied, "We are going to take our country back."

Made in the USA
Monee, IL
03 April 2023